Platirius Infiltration
Book I
D.L. Hannah

D.L. HANNAH

Contents

For my daughter. Never believe the stars are out of your reach. Thank you for being fearless.

Chapter 1

"Why did you bring that thing here?" asked Sindee.

"I didn't," said Sonee. "I took it from the Revaltians."

Sindee raised an eyebrow. "Oh? And where did they find it?"

Sonee kept her eyes on her work. If she didn't finish before Queen Vivant returned, she'd be in huge trouble. "In its home. Earth."

"But that's against the rules! Why would they risk punishment for that?"

"Not sure," said Sonee as she continued experimenting on the silent figure suspended above them. "I think there's something the Humans have that the Revaltians want. I've been scanning its brain, but no luck so far. I'll need a bit more time to figure out why they wanted it."

Sindee took a sip of PotterBerry juice. "Have you asked it?"

"Of course not. Scanning its brain is much faster and more accurate."

Humans hadn't been on Platirius since King Dubian was alive. Whatever the Revaltians wanted with the thing, it was big enough to break protocol and risk exposure. Sonee was nearly delirious with anticipation to solve the mystery. If she did, it was a guaranteed promotion up the ranks. That is, if Queen Vivant didn't have her thrown into the Flames of Justice.

Without reading her mind, Sindee echoed her fears. "If Queen Vivant finds out this thing is here, you'll be punished, regardless of the reason."

Sonee nodded grimly. "I'm aware. Except the Revaltians don't operate without a plan."

Sindee hesitated before continuing. "Did you alert Simonius? Maybe he can help."

Sonee made a face. She didn't particularly like Simonius. He was a handsome MaleForm with impeccable intellectual ability. Yet, there was something about him that made Sonee uneasy. He was too quiet. When he smiled, it was difficult to discern his thoughts and feelings. She felt a creepy vibe whenever she had to interact with him.

Unlike more than a few of the Vivacian soldiers who were enamored by his countenance and articulation, she avoided him. MaleForms, along with Humans, were not to be trusted. Nevertheless, Simonius was the last thing Sonee wanted to discuss.

"No. That would place him at risk, too."

"But that's his assignment," said Sindee.

"Studying. Researching. Yes, I'm aware of his assignment, Sindee. He's been watching these things for millions of years. There's nothing special about Humans. They're selfish, intolerant, and filled with avarice and arrogance. They seek new ways to hate and fight each other over meaningless things. They don't realize there are more superior Beings that could wipe them out in the blink of a star."

"Some of them are aware Beings outside their planet exist. In a place called the United States, their government informed them. *Extraterrestrials,* they call us. After it was revealed, many of them didn't care."

Sonee rolled her eyes. "I'm not surprised. That's why they're easy to defeat. All they care about is food and copulating with each other. A mediocre race if one ever existed."

Sindee eyed her with wonder. "You sound like the Revaltians! Why do you hate them?"

"I don't hate them. I simply don't find anything interesting about them. They watch finite shows while we watch them. To me, they're one big comedic monologue. Nothing more. They can't even protect themselves if a galactic war breaks out. Their planet would be at our mercy."

Sadly shaking her head, Sindee said, "Don't let Queen Vivant hear you say that. She is keen on staying neutral. The Revaltians—not so much. They want to take over Earth in the worst way."

Sonee entered more data into the system. "That's precisely why I have to find out why they kidnapped this thing."

"Who brought this Human to my realm?"

Gasp.

Queen Vivant!

As Queen Revari walked down the long familiar corridor, loathing surged within her. Queen Vivant shouldn't have been crowned. The honor should've solely gone to her. For far too long, she had despised not being the only ruler of the Platirius empire. Her sickening altruism wasn't the kind of leadership Platirius needed.

The Humans could not be trusted. If King Dubian had the gumption to destroy them years ago, they would've added Earth to the collection of planets they'd conquered. But no—he was too focused on taking Coldarius first. That proved to be a grave mistake. Another reason he didn't try to overthrow Earth—he feared The One.

Humans were loved and shielded from the power of galaxy races like the Platirians. Earth would've been routed long ago if it weren't for The One. She narrowed her eyes in disgust. Insects. Vermin. They were worth nothing more than excrement you flushed down the drain.

While other empires continued acquiring knowledge and assimilating among them, King Dubian had abolished Human experimentation on Platirius during his reign. However, his decree hadn't stopped her. She had taken great pleasure in secretly conducting the experiments.

She'd discovered pain was the motivator to get answers. The more they cried out in agony, the more she learned about their planet.

Such a fool he was, she thought. *For many of their years, Humans had experimented on themselves! If they had such little respect for their race, why should Platirians show mercy?*

She paused as she reached the door to her meeting chamber. This was the last place she wanted to be. Summoned to Platineous like a mere servant. The *gall* of Queen Vivant. She was her equal in every way. No—more than that.

Queen Revari was *better* than her. Stronger. Smarter. Faster. Still, Queen Vivant had been hand-picked by King Dubian to rule Platirius while she would be given nothing! Well—she had fixed his little plan, hadn't she? Still, it hadn't gone as she expected.

It didn't matter. She was simply biding her time. Once Queen Vivant was dethroned, she'd own it all one day.

She scanned her hand across the TeleShield, and the door to her meeting chamber opened with a soft *swoosh.*

"Come in," said Queen Vivant without looking up from a stack of documents. She didn't need to. She knew exactly who stood before her. Anytime she met with her, it was never a pleasant experience. Queen Revari wasted no time in proving her right.

"Why have you summoned me?" she asked.

She put down the pen she used to scroll the latest instructions for her army. As she surveyed Queen Revari, she decided not to prologue the meeting. She had a million other issues to address. There was no time to waste.

"A Human has been brought to Platirius. I'd like to know why."

Queen Revari fell silent. It was impossible to scan her impassive gaze to discern if she was the culprit.

"How should I know?" she coolly asked. "And what does it have to do with me?"

"None of my subjects would dare bring a Human here."

Queen Revari chuckled. She moved closer to a TranScreen that held an image of a Human male. "Don't be so sure. You cannot be everywhere at once. And—" She paused to swipe a red, manicured nail across the detailed image of the Human's brain. "—you cannot read my mind."

"You cannot read mine either."

"It's a pity for the Humans that he didn't extend the courtesy to them. I can read every thought they form."

She looked over her shoulder at her. "The Humans. Mere insects. Are they more intelligent than us? Whose race is more superior, us or them? For thousands of their years, all they've done is create wars. They live to fight each other over petty issues. Skin color, whom to pray to, and now? The latest cause of division is whom they copulate with."

Queen Vivant shrugged. "That's how it has always been. My job is to help them, not add to their burdens."

"They invent ways to murder each other but you believe they should be left alone. Before you became The One's pet, you despised them more than I."

Queen Vivant's eyes misted as she expelled a long breath. "I was wrong. Had I not changed my ways, I never would've been appointed as Earth's protector."

Queen Revari stared at her for a long moment. "How foolish of you," she said.

"You will watch your tongue in my presence."

"Or what? What will you do to me? I'm not one of your soldiers! I earned the right to be queen. You? Everything you own was handed to you on a platter. Everyone knows you fail in comparison to me as a queen and a warrior. You may lie to yourself a million times but we both know the truth!"

She leaned forward. "I'm warning you."

Queen Revari closed the distance between them. "I wouldn't. I wouldn't warn me if I were you."

She's trying to intimidate me, thought Queen Vivant. "Did you bring that Human here or not?!"

"No, I didn't. If that's what you wanted to know, you could've used the TranScreen to contact me. I don't like my time being wasted on such frivolous matters."

"The Human isn't the only issue I wanted to discuss."

Queen Revari slammed her hand down on the desk. "Then get to the point! I'm busy."

She didn't flinch. She was used to her quick temper. "I think you are the best suspect for abducting the Human. You subjected them to experiments long after King Dubian forbade it."

Queen Revari laughed. "So? That was years ago. I'm the queen of half of Platirius. I'm much more powerful than I was under King Dubian's oppressive thumb. Why would I bring such a thing here now?"

Does she not know about the Human? thought Queen Vivant. She didn't trust her. She'd stab her own in the back and throw them into the dark abyss of Space without a second thought.

"If that's all you have to say, I'm leaving. You have too much time on your hands to make such wild, baseless accusations."

"A Human female recently saw your half of the planet. Rubarius."

She stopped in mid-stride and turned to her. For the first time, Queen Vivant mused, she seemed utterly thrown off guard.

"Impossible. No Human—female or male—has ever seen Rubarius and lived! I have no use for them!"

Her mind reverted to a younger version of Queen Revari—filled with vitality and an eagerness to love the Humans. Now, there was no trace of her inside the bitter, apathetic WomanForm who stood before her.

"She didn't come through protocol. One of my intelligence agents listened to a live-streamed recording of her. She described Rubarius in great detail and said she saw LifeForms fighting...in a 'street.' We don't have streets—our roads paved in jewels. However, her Human mind would've perceived what she says she saw as precisely that—a street in *public*. She described the temperature radiating off of a red planet. That...is your half of the queendom, Rubarius."

"How?! How could she possibly see Rubarius?"

Queen Vivant sat back in her chair, stretching her long legs. "She was able to see your planet through The One."

"The One?" Queen Revari echoed in disbelief. "Why would He show her Rubarius?"

"That...I do not know."

"The decree says we cannot harm Humans unless they trespass on either side of Platirius. I'd be within my full rights to bring her here for an interrogation. And I will."

As she turned to leave again, Queen Vivant's words stopped her cold. "You cannot bring her in for interrogation. She is protected."

She swung around fiercely. "By WHOM? Who would DARE interfere in My Queendom?"

"The One protects her. And since He does, you aren't permitted to touch her. He would destroy Platirius in the blink of a star. You know this."

Her mind raced wildly.

Why show her Rubarius? Was He planning to empower the Humans to destroy them?

Numerous questions swirled in her mind. There was much to discuss. But not with Queen Vivant. As the appointed Protector of Earth, she helped the Humans far too much with their mental issues. Coddled them. Shielded them from things they'd have no way of coping with.

Queen Revari had refused the appointment. She'd rather die than help the Humans. But now she wanted to know more about the Human female protected by The One. But how? She couldn't question Him. It was forbidden. She needed time to think—and to plan.

She glared at the older queen. "If that's all, I'll be on my way."

Queen Vivant nodded. "That's all I wanted—to know if you were behind this abduction. Now I am satisfied you are not."

"Did this Human see any other planets?"

Queen Vivant pursed her lips. Queen Revari's mind was quick. Too quick.

"I'm not at liberty to discuss—"

Her temper exploded. "Not at liberty to discuss! Do you know who I am? Do you think I'm one of your spineless servants at your beck and call?! I control half of this queendom!"

"And I control the other half. Which means I don't have to share everything that goes on. King Dubian decreed this before he died."

"That's right! He's dead!" *And you should be too*, she thought. However, she didn't dare say it aloud. Queen Vivant would have her arrested for treason. She couldn't risk that now.

She had to find out *how* and *why* the Human female saw Rubarius. And what, if any, connection she had with the Human the Vivacians were holding now. She was so close to executing her plans. She couldn't afford to get caught off guard.

"I'm leaving. My day was off to a good start before you sent for me."

As she whirled around to leave, Queen Vivant's words sent a chill down her spine. "He looks very similar to the Human male you found when we were younger."

She gritted her teeth and spun to face her nemesis with a cool façade. "Never mention him to me. Ever. He's dead. Just like your father, King Dubian!"

As she stormed off, Queen Vivant's soft words were more for her than for Queen Revari.

"King Dubian was your father too, my dear sister."

"**W**hy does she always think we're to blame every time something happens?" asked Cia.

"Because we are," said Cyen. "We brought the male thing here, but Queen Vivant doesn't know that."

"And won't," said Queen Revari perusing Cyen, Cia's twin sister. Cyen and Cia were magicians in the Revaltian army, along with Jia, who was as equally powerful as her teammates.

Queen Revari leaned back, surveying her nails. *Queen Vivant's daughters are having a LifeCelebration for their day of birth. I finally have the opportunity to give them a present their mother will never forget.* "Cyen, the thing is being held in the Outer Realm. I want you to infiltrate his mind. Under your control, he'll do exactly as you command him to."

Cyen leaned forward in anticipation. "Of course, My Queen. Anything for Rubarius."

Queen Revari narrowed her eyes. "I never get tired of hearing that. Now—here's what you're going to do…"

After briefing her team on what was to be done, Queen Revari entered the confinement chamber where the Human male was imprisoned. She surveyed him with a mixture of boredom and disgust.

"Do you know why no MaleForms rule either half of Platirius?"

Kyle eyed her warily. Although he feared her, he tried not to show it. He had to be careful if he wanted to make it out of there alive. This woman was nothing like the other queen. Queen Vivant had barely tolerated him, but at least she was kind. This one was ruthless. Cold. Calculating. She'd kill him without a second thought.

He watched her lips curl into a cold smile. She already knew he was afraid of her. Very afraid.

"No," he said. He figured out MaleForms was what they called the men on their planet. Their strange language was similar to English, but not quite.

"Because MaleForms destroy everything they touch. Just look at your pathetic shell of a planet. Wars are fought on every side of the globe. Hatred. Dissention. Blatant disrespect of your female breed. Human males are jealous of the females, just as MaleForms are jealous of WomenForms. And you're never satisfied. Not with yourselves or each other."

"But don't you get off on that stuff?"

Immediately, he bit the inside of his cheek. "*Be cool, Kyle! Don't tick her off!*"

"Of course. The negativity you spew strengthens me and our cause. Every time one of you descends into mental despair or ends human life—be it your own or another's—I grow more powerful. It's how I've held my own against Queen Vivant. She's tried for far too long to heal your kind. But you're hopeless. Helpless. Pathetic. You were created to serve your betters, nothing more."

"Humans may have our faults, but I assure you, Lady, you're no better than the worst of us!"

He swore softly. His mind told him to be careful, but her arrogance annoyed him. Immediately, a blast of searing pain coursed through his body. He sank to his knees in anguish. It was her! She could inflict pain without touching him!

"Ohhhhhhh God!" he cried out in horror.

She watched as he writhed in agony. "He's not here to save you. You will show me proper respect, insect."

"I'm...sorry," he rasped.

"I APOLOGIZE FOR MY IGNORANCE AND INSOLENCE, QUEEN REVARI!"

"I—I apologize for my—ahhhh—ignorance and insolence, Queen Revari!"

"That's better, insect. Much better."

Fearing he'd set her off again, he kept quiet. He tried to take his mind off the pain, but his blood felt as if it was boiling inside his veins. A burning sensation shot through his head, causing bile to erupt from his throat. If the torment didn't stop soon, he'd pass out. He couldn't let that happen. He had to keep his wits about him.

She scanned his mind. "It honestly doesn't matter if you're awake or asleep. I could kill you in a second. You're no match for me, Kyle Human. None of your kind is. Now that you no longer have Queen Vivant as an ally—well—I'm afraid your time has run out."

"I'm supposed to stand trial!"

She chuckled. "Do you think that will help your plight? Allow me to crush your bit of hope. You'll be found guilty and sentenced to death. There hasn't been a Human male's death on this planet since King Dubian's reign. Nevertheless, I intend to make your death as slow and painful as possible for what you've done."

"You set me up!" he cried.

"Did I?" She drew a noose in the dirt with the tip of her boot. "How?"

He fell silent.

Her slow perusal was filled with unabashed hatred. "Do you think my sister will believe you—a mere Human—over me, a

Platirian? We have footage of you placing the Ashion bulbs inside the gift boxes. Are you that arrogant you don't realize what's happening?"

"I've done nothing wrong."

"Oh, but you have. You never should have come here, Human."

He sat back against the wall, breathing harshly. "I don't know how I got here."

"It's not for you to know." She backed away from him. "But—since I'm such a generous queen, you'll know exactly how you came to Platirius right before you're punished. I'll make certain of that."

King Dubian's Past

King Anemi looked at his son with a mixture of loathing and distaste. Prince Dubian was nothing like him. He was too kind. Too soft. Just like his mother. Over time, it had been easy to ignore the boy. Prince Dubian was his second son—an unwanted ChildForm. He'd never rule Platirius.

That honor would go to Prince Dimaro—the pride of his loins. His firstborn son was the superior hunter and fighter. He was also better at shooting and juggling silly WomenForms—everything he did made King Anemi proud.

Prince Dubian, however, no. Although the boy was a good fighter, his skills would never surpass his brother, no matter how hard he tried. Now, the young prince was stammering in a way that irritated King Anemi. Would he ever be masculine enough to look him in the eye?

"I cannot understand a single thing you're whining about!" he snapped. "Out with it already!"

He swallowed hard. He wasn't his father's favorite, which made having a decent conversation with him more challenging. He avoided his father whenever possible. The motherless young prince had just entered primary school when he'd finally summoned the courage to ask about her. Immediately, King Anemi made him wish he hadn't.

"Your mother was a witless, silly WomanForm. A classless whore who was beyond easy to lie with. And in one lustful, drunken night, you were conceived. After you killed her in childbirth, I banished all knowledge of her from the Memory of Records. I don't regret lying with her. She was skilled, and I was young, ready to sow my oats wherever I pleased. That—Prince Dubian—is what WomenForms are for. They have no purpose other than to breed and heed to every whim of MaleForms."

King Anemi got up and stared out of a window. "They're whiny. Bratty. Unintelligent. The only thing they're good for is spreading their legs. Nothing more. She thought I cared for her. A commoner! Why, the very idea was preposterous! My wife wanted to raise you, so I allowed it. But don't you think for one second I hold you in the same regard as Prince Dimaro."

Turning back to look at him, he said, "Your brother is the rightful heir to Platirius. When my time has passed, he will lead Platirius into an even finer kingdom than I've created. Under my leadership, it has become second only to the realm of The One."

The king's lips curled in distaste. "In your hands, it would be just as pitiful as that subpar planet, Earth. You don't have what it takes to be a leader. You haven't even had your first piece of pleasure. Although your acumen for battle is—adequate, what would you know about commanding an army?"

He finally raised his head and looked at King Anemi. "I am saving myself," he said.

The king raised an eyebrow. "Saving yourself?" he echoed. "Saving yourself for what?"

"For Princess Dellah," said Prince Dubian.

Incredulous, he gawked at his second son before laughing in his face.

Prince Dubian didn't like that. Not one bit. But having a duplicitous nature had proven to be beneficial for him. If his father thought he was weak and feeble-minded, that was fine with him. His ignorance would give him an advantage in succeeding with his plans.

Prince Dubian kept his temper in check while the king coughed and sputtered before wiping tears from his eyes.

He surveyed the prince in wonderment. "Do you think King Carlomon would allow you—a simpleton—to marry his daughter?"

He laughed harder. "Son, you are forgetting yourself. You're a prince, yes. But you are a second prince. You don't get to decide whom you marry. Second-born sons have always followed tradition and married Breeders. Breeders produce soldiers. Unlike the ChildForms of Firstborns, they receive no inheritance. Their purpose is to fight and die."

His icy gaze bore into him. "That is their fate and their duty to Platirius. A young, supple, beautiful creature such as Princess Dellah deserves to be on the arm of a Firstborn so she may give him strong sons to carry out his legacy. King Carlomon wouldn't spit on you if you spontaneously burst into flames."

Inwardly, he fumed, but kept his face impassive. Prince Dimaro would NOT marry Princess Dellah. She loved *him,* and he loved her even more fiercely. He'd gut him and spit on his carcass before he allowed him to marry her. And his father too. But—King Anemi didn't know that. And wouldn't—until it was too late.

The king waved his hand. He'd heard enough.

"Go away. I'm done with this foolishness. Your bride will be selected from the Breeders." Narrowing his eyes, he said, "You will be happy with my choice or you'll be exiled from Platirius. And by the galaxy, you won't last an hour alone. You'll die. The way you should've died in your mother's womb. Now leave me." He waved his hand as if swatting away a fly.

"Sergeant!" he barked.

Immediately, Sergeant Quito appeared. 'Yes, King Anemi!"

"Call my beloved son. We have much to discuss."

"Right away, My King!"

With false cheerfulness, he forced himself to bow. "I bid you a good day, Father. Thank you for always providing such wonderful advice."

King Anemi ignored him as he exited his meeting chamber.

Out of his father's sight, he finally allowed his anger to consume him. The audacity of that decrepit old fool! For seventeen years, he'd endured his father's cruelty. He'd been overlooked and underappreciated. Nothing he did was ever good enough for him.

Once, he'd beaten Prince Dimaro in a duel, but their father had called the honor in his brother's favor. He couldn't admit he wasn't the feeble-minded weakling he painted him as. It had been a mistake to mention Princess Dellah. Now that King Anemi was aware of his feelings, he'd make it his mission to thwart his plans.

She was the only source of light in his short, miserable life. After he met her, everything changed. He didn't feel so lonely. So despised. She was everything he'd ever wanted. Beautiful—inside and out. She exuded a positivity he'd never experienced before. She never sneered or looked down her nose at anyone.

She treated everyone in her father's kingdom fairly, from the lowest of servants to the highest rank of soldiers. No matter how ridiculous, dreams of having her as a wife had kept him going.

Some MaleForms simply wanted to marry a king's daughter. She was the most coveted WomanForm in the galaxy. She would be a feather in Prince Dimaro's cap—nothing more. He wasn't in love with her, nor did he care about her love of poetry or how she wore her hair.

His brother wouldn't spend time eating with her in the royal gardens or hold her hand when she was upset. He would. He'd be damned if he allowed King Anemi to change the fate of their future. He would marry Princess Dellah and make her his queen. But first—his father had to die.

Queen Revari's Past

Princess Revari entered the medical chamber where King Dubian lay dying. The day she'd waited for had finally arrived. In a few moments, he would be no more. Her sister's absence from Platirius had granted her the perfect opportunity. Princess Vivant had the power to heal and restore health to any Being in the galaxy, but she had been too young when their mother died to preserve her life.

Queen Dellah had died while giving birth to her. And he'd never allowed her to forget it. Unlike Princess Vivant, Princess Revari was denied the right to have LifeCelebrations.

"Why would I celebrate the day you murdered my wife?" At only two years old, his bitter words tore deeply into his young daughter's psyche. The little princess thought her heart would break in half. None of the servants had dared to tell her what happened to her mother.

They were too afraid of her father. Even Princess Vivant hadn't known the cause of Queen Dellah's death. He'd forbidden anyone to speak of it. Anyone who disobeyed his order would've faced execution. He looked coldly down at his second daughter, unmoved by the tears silently flowing from her eyes.

"When my wife told me she was carrying again, I tried to convince her to rid her body of you. We already had Princess Vivant—the best daughter any king could have. We didn't need a second ChildForm. But she wouldn't hear of it. She had your nursery chamber elaborately decorated and for what? She never had the chance to see it in completion. I would trade your death a thousand times over hers. You've been nothing but a thorn in my side. You are a pathetic waste of space."

A shocked gasp interrupted his quiet tirade. No one on Platirius had ever heard him raise his voice. He hadn't needed to. His tongue was venomous, skilled at cutting down whoever was on the receiving end of it. A gift he'd inherited from his father, King Anemi. He looked up to see a NurseForm looking at him in horror. Quickly, she dropped her startled gaze in fear.

"Get her out of my sight," he said through gritted teeth. "Make sure she doesn't cross my path unless I send for her."

"Yes, King Dubian." She hurried quickly over to the young princess, who was now shaking as racking sobs penetrated her petite form. Scooping her into her arms, the NurseForm promptly took her into her nursery chamber.

"Your father didn't mean what he said, Princess Revari. He's still hurting over your mother's death."

But the young princess didn't believe the NurseForm. Deep in her heart, she knew her father had meant every word he'd spoken to her. A tiny seed of hatred began to grow in her mind.

Chapter 2

M any years later, her hatred of King Dubian had grown into an uncontrollable blaze. As he'd done with King Anemi, Princess Revari was careful in hiding her true nature from him.

Now that he was dying, she intended for him to know exactly how she felt. That, she decided, was the best part. Oh—how she savored the moment. She'd finally have revenge for all the pain he'd caused throughout her life.

"How are you feeling, King Dubian?" While Princess Vivant had called him Father, he never allowed her to. Over time, she'd stopped caring.

"I feel as if the biggest craft in the universe has run over me. I'll be delighted once Princess Vivant returns to heal me. There are so many things I have to do to expand Platirius's borders."

Oh, don't worry, she thought. *That responsibility will be mine now.*

He looked at his youngest daughter and frowned. He truly regretted the way he had treated her. Although she'd grown up to be as beautiful as her mother, she was cold, withdrawn, and extremely ruthless. She was a skilled warrior in Platirius's army.

She never complained if she was hurt in battle, which wasn't often.

An expert in fighting the best MaleForm warriors in the galaxy, she'd taken more than a few heads of generals and princes. Her mother would have been very proud of her. He only hoped his beloved queen would forgive him when he saw her again.

"I've never noticed—but you look exactly like your mother."

"Do I?" At the mention of Queen Dellah, the last bit of her patience vanished like a puff of smoke. The careful façade she'd cultivated over time broke like a dam.

For years, he'd treated her as something he'd scraped from the bottom of his boot. Since he'd never shared any memories of her mother with her, she wasn't impressed or moved by his compliment.

"Well—I'm afraid it's too late for sentiments, Father."

He let out a harsh cough, his eyes bulged when a foul purple substance spewed from his throat.

"Oh dear!" she said, dramatically covering her mouth. "I mean King Dubian. I've never been permitted to call you Father, have I?" She smiled coldly. "I took a page out of your book. After all, you murdered your father too, didn't you?"

She stared down at him as he writhed in pain. "I've certainly learned from the best. You. To get what you want, first, you have to get rid of the enemy! How did I do, My King? Is this an accomplishment you're finally proud of?"

"What—did you do to me?"

She shrugged. "It was simple. I had some of the Ashion flower crushed into your food. You really shouldn't have sent Princess Vivant away for training. Now there's no one here to help you. You cannot imagine how much I'm enjoying watching you die."

He tried to call for help but couldn't. The Ashion made it difficult to breathe.

"You've made me so miserable over the years," she seemed to say more to herself than the MaleForm dying in front of her. "Finally, I get to spit in your cold, decrepit face."

He stared at her as if he'd never seen her before. "Reve?" he asked.

She narrowed her eyes, perfectly imitating the look he gave when he threatened others. "You dare to refer to me by that? After what you did to me? To *him*? Even in dying, you show me no respect!"

She circled him like a lioness over prey. "We both know how you feel about me. You never loved me! Never accepted me! You always blamed me for Mother's death! You never let me forget I was the unwanted ChildForm. Princess Vivant was the apple of your eye. For all of your whining about the injustices inflicted upon you by your father, you're just like him! You never treated me any better than he treated you!"

"You killed my wife," he said, coughing rapidly. "The love of my life. What did you expect?"

"Die, you cold-hearted monster! I hope you never see Mother again. Hell is too good for you!"

He tried to sit up and fell back, breathing harshly. The poisonous Ashion swiftly coursed through his body, shutting down his organs. He knew he was going to die. He wasn't ready! The little brat had deceived him. He should've known her little shows of concern were just that—performances.

She'd never shown she cared about anyone except for herself. He never imagined she'd murder him! And Princess Vivant—what would happen to her and her daughters? Would she kill them as well? What would become of Platirius?

She read his mind and smiled smugly. "Oh, don't worry. Platirius will be in excellent hands—mine! I'm not sharing anything with your favorite daughter. Now that her husband is gone and you're on your way out, no one can protect her."

"Your sister isn't as fragile as you think she is. Kindness isn't a weakness. That's something you've never been able to understand."

She cocked her head to one side. "Well, I had a good instructor on that one, didn't I? You never showed me an ounce of kindness. It's far too late to talk about it now. Especially for you."

He clutched his chest. "She loves you. But she won't forgive you for what you've done."

"Who's going to tell her? *I* am not as dumb as *you* think I am! It will look as if you died of natural causes. And if he doesn't want to end up dead and shipped into the heart of the sun right along with your rotting corpse, that's exactly what the chief royal physician will write in his report!"

All too soon, the light started dimming for King Dubian. His throat swelled up so tightly that he could no longer speak. He cursed himself for underestimating her. In the distance, he thought he saw his beloved queen walking towards him with her arms outstretched.

He opened his arms, welcoming her embrace. Suddenly, she became a hideous beast with glowing eyes and sharp fangs. A scream died on his lips as his body went limp.

"Farewell, King Dubian," said Princess Revari. "Off to the gates of Hell you go!"

On cue, the medical team rushed in and began properly disposing of his corpse. Dr. Barrios, the chief royal physician, met her eyes and nodded. She knew he wouldn't dare challenge her. He'd do precisely as instructed. When Princess Vivant returned, the second part of her plan would unfold.

Suddenly, there was an enormous shift in the atmosphere, followed by a loud noise. She and the medical team cried out in shock. The ground beneath their feet began shaking violently. Strange, blinding colors flowed through the air. She screamed.

What in the galaxy is happening?

Shielding her eyes from the unrelenting hues, she heard a loud, ripping sound. Then, a massive blow to the head sent her spiraling into darkness.

S he felt her stomach go queasy as she opened her eyes. Slowly, she struggled to her feet, her head still throbbing. As she strained her eyes against a strange light, her eyes widened in fear. She couldn't believe what she saw.

Quickly, she ran from the medical chamber and saw King Dubian's body lying in an odd strip of darkness. Beyond that—the ground was *platinum*? She looked past him and saw grand, platinum architecture nestled by miniature structures made of platinum, chrome, and diamonds.

However, the ground she stood on was a deep crimson. She whirled around and saw an equally sizable, splendidly built palace standing behind her. It was red and encased in luxurious gold and sparkling rubies. She marveled at the spectacular gardens surrounding it.

She noted smaller buildings of equal majestic beauty. To her amazement, fish covered in gold, diamonds, and rubies jumped up and dove back into clear, cool pools at the palace's base. For the first time, she was at a loss for words.

A voice rang out from the stars. "Queen Revari! You have murdered your father, King Dubian. As a consequence, the kingdom of Platirius has been split into equal realms. Platirius was created from fierce battles resulting in an amalgamation of other realms. For millions of years, it has been ruled by a single king. When King Dubian acquired the planet Coldarius, Platirius became the sprawling force it is now."

Queen Revari looked around. "It didn't split when King Dubian murdered King Anemi. Why now?"

"The galaxy's laws are just, Queen Revari," the voice said gently. "Now, for the first time in history, the control of Platirius will be shared between you and Queen Vivant. You are the first WomanForm ruler of one half of Platirius—Rubarius. It is the land on which you stand. Queen Vivant is the first WomanForm ruler of the other half—Platineous. All of the platinum land and everything on it is under her authority. You control everything past the crimson borders."

Her fists clenched. "What?! That isn't fair! I've earned the right to be queen, not Vivant!"

"No, Queen Revari. You haven't earned the throne. You've taken it."

She glared defiantly at the stars. "So did King Dubian!"

"Yes, he did. However, there was no on Platirius to share the throne."

She closed her eyes in disbelief, forcing herself to remain calm. Throwing a tantrum wasn't going to help her now. She pointed to the stretch of darkness. "What is that strip of land where King Dubian lies?"

"That—is neutral ground," said the voice. "It is called the Outer Realm. It belongs to neither you or Queen Vivant. Visitors may land on it, but they are not permitted to stay. You may remove any Beings on the strip and return them to their rightful planet. You cannot punish them unless they trespass on Rubarius or Platineous. It is simply a matter of which side finds the visitors first."

Heaven itself won't save anyone foolish enough to enter my territory.

She peered into the stars, trying to find the source of the voice.

"Think of it as—on a micro-level scale of cognitive comprehension—an airport. It is merely a place to arrive and leave Platirius. Anyone may end up on it. Thanks to you, King Dubian lies there and will be leaving very soon. You and Queen Vivant must make funeral preparations and dispose of his vessel."

She trained her eyes on King Dubian's corpse and smiled.

"Also, you both possess all of the power King Dubian inherited from the past rulers of Platirius. You have the ability to read and control the minds of other LifeForms, yet not the minds of each other. While this wasn't an issue for a single ruler, now that Platirius has two, mind probing and mind control would give one a decisive and unfair advantage. Upon her return, we will also advise Queen Vivant of the new changes."

Had she'd known Platirius would split, she would've killed them both. For now, she'd play the game until she had her sister where she wanted her—underneath her heel.

"Each of you will have an army of soldiers and magicians under your control. You may choose a name for your army."

Queen Revari didn't hesitate. "The Revaltians."

"Very good. Earth is the only planet in the galaxy that will reunite Platirius under one authority. If you conquer it and more than half of its LifeForms, Platirius will be yours. However, as Queen Vivant has been named the Protector of Earth, she won't stand by and allow this to happen. A new leader will be appointed if you and Queen Vivant expire before Earth is overthrown. We must warn you, the new head of Platirius will come from your rival planet, Kikhani."

"A Kikhanian ruling over Platirians!" she exclaimed. "That's absolute perversion! We *despise* them. They must never have it!"

"There's another way. If you or Queen Vivant births a purebred MaleForm, Platirius will reunite on its power under his reign."

She firmly shook her head. "No. There will be no more MaleForm leaders. I want it all! I want to control everyone and everything on Platirius and Earth!"

"Good luck to you then. As your ancestors before you, you are responsible for quelling planets alone. You will receive no assistance from us."

She scowled at the stars. "Who are you?"

"We are the Surveyors. We watch everything that goes on in the galaxy. Our position is solely to provide information when essential. However, we are never permitted to help any side."

"The information you've provided is crucial to expanding my power. More than you know."

She had taken excellent care planning for King Dubian's execution and had enjoyed watching him die. Immensely. She hadn't come this far only to share Platirius with *Queen Vivant.*

She grimaced. Referring to her as *queen* nearly made her violently ill. Platirius would be hers, no matter the cost. Drawing her attention to King Dubian's cold vessel, she knew precisely what she must do to make it happen.

Queen Vivant's past

As her craft dipped closer to Platirius, Princess Vivant couldn't shake the feeling that something was wrong.

"Be at ease, Princess Vivant," said Colonel Lyric. "Princess Revari is no match for King Dubian. She'd be a fool to challenge his authority."

"Yes, I know. But it's so strange. I cannot feel father's presence. I've only had this feeling when my mother died. I could no longer sense her presence. Now, it's happening again."

"Princess Revari may be ruthless, but even she isn't cold enough to kill her father."

Princess Vivant shuddered. "I hope you're right."

Perhaps Colonel Lyric wasn't right, she thought as she looked down at King Dubian's body.

His face was contorted in an odd grimace. She didn't know how he died, but she suspected he didn't go peacefully. There was one Platirian who knew exactly what happened. She intended to learn the truth from Princess Revari.

As she turned to leave, a voice called, "Queen Vivant!"

Startled, she turned in its direction. "Yes? I am Princess Vivant."

"No, not anymore. Upon King Dubian's death, you have been appointed queen."

"The queen of Platirius," she whispered.

"No," the voice corrected. "You are now the queen of Platineous."

She peered into the stars. "What in the galaxy is Platineous? And who are you?" she asked.

"Platineous is your realm to rule. We are the Surveyors. Step into the light," they said.

With Colonel Lyric at her side, she moved closer to the musical sound and gasped. Just as Queen Revari had witnessed only moments ago, she eyed an enormous edifice of platinum and diamonds. Luscious fruit and vegetation flourished in smaller, intricate buildings.

The sweet perfume of beautiful flowers filled her nostrils. Everywhere she looked was brilliant, platinum beauty. Platirius had been stunning, but even its glory couldn't rival this.

She looked across the strange strip of darkness where she stood with King Dubian's body and saw another equally beautiful kingdom covered in rubies, gold, and precious stones.

"What happened here?" she asked breathlessly.

And so, the Surveyors informed her of everything they'd told Queen Revari—except how King Dubian died. As far as she knew, he'd succumbed to a mysterious illness. Overwhelmed with guilt for not being around to restore his health in time, she hung her head and wept.

Colonel Lyric embraced her. "This isn't your fault. He sent you to training. There was nothing you could do."

"I should've been here."

"Sheer nonsense! Were you to disobey a king's order? You know better than that, My Queen."

She wiped her eyes and looked towards the stars. "But why did Platirius split into two realms?"

"Although Queen Revari has been a faithful warrior for Platirius, she is reckless, ruthless, unkind, and has a fiery temper. Crimson personifies her powers more accurately. The hue of your healing powers is deeply rooted in all that is good and kind in Platirius. Your powers represent platinum. Galaxy law does not permit you to rule Platirius together. You may now choose a name for your army."

"My army will be called the Vivacians. I appoint Colonel Lyric as my general."

"Fair enough. Long ago, before King Dubian was born, Platineous and Rubarius were two planets conquered by your ancestors. Both belong to a long line of ancient planets that shaped Platirius into what it is today. Before it's downfall, Rubarius was built upon most of the negative energy in the universe. King Barron was a vicious leader who showed no mercy to LifeForms. When his reign ended, his essence was so profoundly interwoven into Rubarius that no one could separate it from the crevices of the planet. Queen Revari's mindset aligns very closely with his."

Queen Vivant and General Lyric looked at each other. "It seems you know my sister well, Surveyors."

"We do. We have watched you both grow and mature. During the split, her energy connected with the dormant power of King Barron, thus resurrecting Rubarius. While your destiny is restoration, hers is aligned with destruction and corruption through the acquisition of great power."

She nodded. "Then the galaxy's only alternative was to split Platirius into two separate queendoms."

"You are correct. Although the king's antics were sometimes questionable, your mother's grace and wisdom balanced Platirius. Queen Dellah's planet was Coldarius, a deep, vibrant blue. Blue is the universal hue of peace. When he destroyed Coldarius, its blue wove deep into the heart of Platirius. You have your mother's heart, while Queen Revari is more similar to your father than even she realizes. We must inform you she plans to rejoin Platirius as a single planet. For her to be successful in this endeavor, she must be the first to subjugate the most coveted planet of all the realms—Earth. If this happens, Platirius will be hers alone to rule. You and your army will be subject to her reign."

"How can I stop her?" asked Queen Vivant.

"We are not permitted to tell you how to defeat her," said the Surveyors. "However, we know how Earth can be subdued. The one who takes Earth will control the minds of most of its inhabitants. Her most potent weapons are afflictions. Exacerbating the negative aspects of life against Humans will create more havoc on the planet. Mental disorders, fear, and negative energy already plague Humans. She may seek to use these against them."

Her heart sank. They'd just lost their father. The last thing she wanted was to enter into a battle with her sister.

"She has the freedom to change her mind and become a Protector instead of a conqueror. If this happens, this is another way Platirius will become one again, with her being second in command of your reign."

"She'll never agree to that," said Queen Vivant.

"This is true," said the Surveyors. "Her birthright revolves around selfish ambition. It has been foretold of Heaven and Hell's roles in the unfolding saga on Earth. The final war between Heaven and Hell must not be interfered with. Your position is a servant in The One's army. What He has deemed precious in His sight, you must preserve. Therefore, Queen Vivant, Earth cannot fall."

"You've given me much to think about at this difficult hour. I thank you, Surveyors."

"We wish you luck."

She stood silently for a moment, processing all the Surveyors had told her. "General Lyric?"

"Yes, My Queen."

"Organize my Vivacians. We need to prepare for King Dubian's DeathCeremony. Also, we have to stop Queen Revari from getting her hands on Earth."

"For Platirius!" said General Lyric.

For the first time since discovering her father's body, Queen Vivant felt a bit hopeful.

"For Platirius!" she said, returning General Lyric's smile.

The Present

Queen Vivant and her subjects happily planned to give her daughters the grandest LifeCelebration ever. Everyone in the queendom, from chefs to stylists, had worked fervently to make delicious and elaborate creations.

No expense had been spared for the princesses. Although it should have been one of the happiest moments of her life, she was uneasy. She didn't know how to explain why she was anxious. She simply was.

General Lyric ran a tight ship. However, not even she could keep watch on everything the Revaltians did. Queen Revari never attended celebratory events on Platineous. Instead, she made trips to other planets, causing as much chaos as possible.

She sighed. She'd never understand why she and her sister were so different.

Even when they were ChildForms, Queen Revari had enjoyed bringing misery to others. When the first Human male arrived at Platirius many years ago, she'd broken the rules and was severely punished for her deeds. Yet, she hadn't changed her ways. Punishment had only worsened her behavior.

After she was freed, her hatred of Humans nearly consumed her. Queen Vivant had tried to get her to see reason. To understand how privileged she was to be a royal figure of such a fine planet.

Queen Revari wasn't interested in being comforted or expressing gratitude. She wanted revenge. She crushed anyone who dared to get in her way. Very few challenged her and that's precisely how she liked it. The sound of her daughter's excited chatter penetrated her thoughts.

"Oh, Mother! Look at the decorations! This is going to be the most awesome LifeCelebration ever!" said Princess Teenah, the firstborn of the triplets.

She quickly banished all thoughts of her sister and the Revaltians. She'd discover how the Human came to their planet, but now wasn't the time.

She wanted to focus on ensuring her daughters had a wonderful celebration of sixteen lifespans. The excitement and wonder in the eyes of her beautiful daughter made her smile.

"Oh, I don't know about that. You and your sisters still have many lifespans left for me to throw extravagant celebrations.

But surprise celebrations are surprises for a reason. You're not supposed to be poking around."

Princess Teenah hugged her mother fiercely. "I know, I know! I just wanted to see!"

"Well, *see* yourself out of here and allow us to finish," she said, returning her hug. "And don't tell your sisters."

"Hmm—do I get to open a present now if I don't?"

The queen pointed to the door. "Out, you little negotiator!"

"Okay, okay! I'm going! And I won't spill the tea! Goodbye, Mother!"

Another wave of uneasiness fell over her. "No, don't say goodbye. Say 'in a while.' You know goodbye is too final for me."

"Father wrote goodbye to you in a letter before his last battle, right?"

Not trusting her voice, she merely nodded.

The princess surveyed her mother carefully. Throughout their life, she had fiercely protected her and her sisters. She wouldn't tell her if something was wrong, especially not today. Although the triplets knew their parents had been deeply in love, they had never known their father.

He was killed in battle as a young MaleForm, leaving a young Queen Vivant to raise the triplets without him. She wished he were here to celebrate with their family. She'd never forgotten her first and only great love.

General Lucian Kron was the most feared warrior in all of the galaxy. Tall, rugged, and exceptionally handsome, his battles were memorialized in the Great Halls of War.

According to legend, he had instantly fallen in love with Princess Vivant. They'd met at King Dubian's thirty-ninth LifeCelebration. His head was still spinning long after he'd retired for the night.

Before her, no WomanForm had captured his attention. She cared deeply about Platirius and its LifeForms. Her passionate speech about living in peace with the rest of the galaxy had won his heart. In all of his lifespan, he'd never met anyone like her. He wanted see her dream of peace come to fruition.

He had asked King Dubian for her hand, but the cold-hearted king would not allow his beloved daughter to marry easily.

At first, he had tried to discourage him from wanting to marry her, but General Kron stood firm.

"It is Princess Vivant I want."

King Dubian narrowed his eyes. He possessed a tremendous amount of respect for the young general for winning countless battles for Platirius. Having him as a son-in-law would be another feather in his cap. However, he wasn't about to let him know that.

Being the sly, cunning creature he was, he posed a proposition. "I intend to finalize conquering Coldarius very soon. As you know, it's my wife's birth planet."

Shortly after Queen Dellah passed, he'd married her twin sister, Opal. According to gossip, he had married her because he couldn't let the memory of his first wife go. Opal had ignored the rumors. She didn't love him either.

She married him for the power and prestige of being a queen. As long as he didn't ask her to share his bed chamber, their arrangement suited her perfectly.

"She's spoken of having her extended family closer to her for years. This is my way of making it happen."

He handed him a glass. "Kron, if you help me secure Coldarius, in seven years, I'll give you Princess Vivant's hand in marriage."

He paused. "If you conquer Coldarius, how many guard posts will you need to set up there?"

"None," said King Dubian.

His grip tightened around the glass. "None?" he echoed. "We need guard stations to manage the LifeForms who live on Coldarius."

"After I conquer it, they won't live there. Coldarius will be absorbed into Platirius. When that happens, Platirius will be the strongest force in the galaxy. Then, I intend to find a way to invade Earth. Acquiring Earth will make Platirius unstoppable and indestructible."

"King Dubian, you can't bring one hundred billion LifeForms to Platirius! Even we don't have enough space for everyone to live comfortably."

The king turned to look him in the eyes. "I said I wanted my wife's family closer to her. I never said I'd bring every LifeForm on Coldarius here."

He stood still. "You mean you're going to kill every Coldarian who isn't related to Queen Opal?!"

King Dubian nodded as if they were discussing no more than an insect landing on a flower. "I don't need them all. Outside of her family members—those who haven't irritated me—I'll bring in more than enough to keep the economy thriving."

"Soldiers and staff."

His sinister black eyes bore into him. "Yes, but that's all we'll need. Anyone left on Coldarius after its energy is absorbed will die. Without energy, they'll all freeze to death. Oh, come now, General Kron! They'll freeze in a matter of hours. It's not as if their deaths will be prolonged."

"But the WomenForms! The InfantForms and ChildForms!" exclaimed General Kron.

"Are insignificant burdens I will take no responsibility to feed and clothe," said King Dubian coldly.

He stared at him in amazement. He'd never liked him. Never trusted him. He was fully aware of how King Dubian had advanced. Becoming king wasn't his birthright. He'd stolen it from his brother.

He loved Platirius. It was his home. He was a true patriot and would do anything to see it thrive. King Dubian's cruel and vicious words rang sharply of his true nature. He wondered how he'd been able to hide his callousness from Queen Opal.

Unlike his marriage to Queen Dellah, their union was strictly for political gain. King Carlomon had allowed Opal to marry him if he expanded Coldarius's borders. Then, both kingdoms would reap the benefits of Platirius's booming economy.

Now, the selfish and greedy king sought to betray his unsuspecting wife and father-in-law. He intended to murder billions of innocent LifeForms on her home planet. If she learned of his plans—she'd stop him.

The king eyed him suspiciously. "You're in no position to tell Queen Opal anything. Or Princess Vivant. That's one of the conditions for you to marry my daughter. The second is helping me acquire Coldarius."

Giving him a crafty smile, he said, "Once we take Coldarius, you'll be the most famous and powerful warrior in the galaxy. How would Princess Vivant feel if she knew you murdered innocent WomenForms and ChildForms in the name of power? She'd spit in your face before you finished asking for her hand."

His bewildered expression dissolved into impassiveness. Revealing his disgust would be treasonous to the throne. He didn't like his methods. His penchant for cruelty had made him the most infamous and despised king in the galaxy.

When he passed, Platirians bowed their heads in fear, not respect. As his father before him, they seldom met his eyes while in his presence.

That was not the legacy he wanted to leave behind when his lifespan expired. Yes, wars were necessary to acquire planets and power, but the sanctity of life should never be an afterthought. King Dubian had no such sentiments.

According to well-kept gossip, he'd murdered his father and brother. General Kron seldom entertained rumors. Yet, he didn't doubt anything he'd heard about Princess Vivant's father.

Still, he knew he had no choice in the matter. His position as general called for unquestionable loyalty to Platirius. Innocent LifeForms would be lost, and there was nothing he could do to stop it.

And Princess Vivant—by the Saints in The One's army, he couldn't bear for her to hate him. King Dubian had him at a disadvantage. For now.

"My services are at your command, My King."

Chapter 3

P rincess Teenah had her father's walk. She watched her
beloved daughter bounce away in anticipation of the
impending festivities. She knew she'd run straight to her sisters
and tell them about the preparations. She chuckled. If you had
a secret, Princess Teenah was the last WomanForm you'd tell.

As the LifeCelebration entered its second hour, Queen Vivant
planned to give the culinary staff and royal decorators a nice
bonus in pay. Both teams worked together and had truly
outdone themselves. The platinum, white, and blue decorations
complemented the vast halls of the dining chamber well.

Platinum table coverings of the softest material sheathed
heavy chrome tables laden with delicious food and drink. She sat
at the head of the table, happily watching her daughters enjoy all
the luxuries she afforded them.

The young WomenForms squealed in delight as a high
seven-layer cake frosted in platinum, white, and blue was
brought to the table. Forty-eight sparklers decorated the top of
the cake, creating a magnificent view.

After it was set down, platinum fireworks burst into Space,
peppering the stars with brilliant light and dazzling colors. Her

smile broadened at the tears of joy nestling in their eyes. It was a beautiful moment. She looked forward to many more.

She nodded to the royal baker to begin slicing the cake. Bowls of thick, rich custard and stewed fruit complimented the luscious, not cloyingly sweet icing.

After a while, Princess Tarah, the middle triplet, threw back her head and groaned. "I can't eat another bite! But it's so good!"

Princess Tyre, the youngest triplet, nodded in agreement with her sister. "We've had amazing LifeCelebrations over the years, but this is the best cake I've ever eaten. I'll be lucky to fit into my nightwear after this."

Suddenly, Princess Teenah frowned and set down her fork. "Mother," she began hesitantly. "Isn't Aunt Reve coming?"

"Oh, come on!" scoffed Princess Tarah. "We're having a lovely time! Why do you have to go and mention her?"

Princess Tyre interjected, "Obviously, she didn't want to be here, and I don't care!"

"That's not fair," said Princess Teenah. "Aunt Reve loves us. She's never received the love we have. Grandmother passed when she was a baby, and Grandfather was—busy—"

"He had a kingdom to rule," said Princess Tyre pointedly. "It's not as if she's been on her own. She had Mother just as we've all had. She's never wanted her love or her help. I'm not going to waste my LifeCelebration talking about Aunt Reve. She's creepy and evil! I'm glad she didn't come!"

"Triplets." Her soft, commanding voice silenced any future argument. "Today is a celebration of your lives. We won't waste a minute of it discussing things we cannot control. Have I been heard?"

"Yes, Mother," said the princesses.

Although their mother was significantly kinder than their aunt, her quiet, powerful nature did not tolerate challenges.

Her stern look vanished. "Now? It's time to open your gifts!"

"Yay!" exclaimed Princess Tarah.

Each princess had sixteen boxes each to open. After loads of jewelry, perfume, and candies were ooooed and ahhed over, the fifteenth gift boxes revealed three elaborate controllers.

"Mother!" exclaimed Princess Teenah. "Are these what I think they are?"

"Well, it's time you learned to navigate your way around the galaxy. Look up at the TranScreen."

Immediately, three shiny new crafts appeared. The princesses let out a series of yells and whoops. Princess Tyre jumped out of her chair and threw herself into Queen Vivant's outstretched arms.

"Mother! We're going to DRIVE! I can't believe it!" she said happily.

"Believe it. You're excellent daughters." As mother and daughters lovingly embraced, she said, "You have set a good example for the young WomenForms of Platineous. They idolize you. You listen well to instructions and finish your lessons without complaints. It brings me joy to provide you with these. I expect you to listen to Sergeant Thea when she provides driving lessons. Is that understood?"

With excitement shining in their eyes, the triplets agreed.

"I can't WAIT!" said Princess Teenah.

"Me either," said Princess Tarah. "But we have one more present to open."

"Well, let's hurry up so we can go!" said Princess Tyre. "I want to see my craft!"

In rapid succession, the princesses opened the final gifts.

"Oh," said Princess Tarah. "It's a beautiful flower!" Each princess removed the flowers from the gift boxes and smelled them.

"This smells wonderful," said Princess Tyre. Suddenly, she swayed. "Mother? What's happening?"

"Ohhhh, I don't feel so well," said Princess Teenah.

Princess Tarah had a strange look on her face. Suddenly, her eyes glazed over as a dark purple, frothy liquid bubbled from her lips.

Queen Vivant jumped to her feet. "Daughters?! What's wrong?!" Looking around wildly, she cried, "Summon the royal physicians!"

"Blow the horns," commanded General Lyric as she rushed to assist the princesses.

Queen Vivant screamed as she ran to Princess Tarah, catching her before she fell to the ground. One by one, the sisters sank to the floor.

In an instant, a wave of panic erupted over the dining chamber. The guests began screaming and crying uncontrollably.

"Silence," she screamed.

Not another sound was made when Platineous's chief royal physician, Dr. Challah, entered with her staff. Quickly, she checked their vital signs.

"We have to get them to the medical chamber now!"

The medical staff lifted them onto stretchers and hurried out of the dining chamber.

"Faster!" cried Dr. Challah. "We're losing them!"

The queen felt the chamber spinning as she ran behind her daughters.

This can't be happening! Not again!

She'd already lost her father and her husband. She couldn't lose her babies. She didn't know how she'd survive without them.

A strange darkness fell over the queendom of Platineous as she sat beside her daughters. Dr. Challah bowed to her. "I'm sorry, Queen Vivant. We've lost them all."

The princesses lay perfectly still on the cool, chrome tables. Except for the slight grimaces etched on their faces, they looked as if they were sleeping. Queen Vivant had often sat in their bed chamber, watching them sleep.

She tried to recall the number of times she'd awakened them with smiles and joyous hugs. Now, they'd never open their eyes again. She struggled to make sense of it.

"By the Heavens!" said General Lyric. "No!"

"They were poisoned." Dr. Challah continued. "Deeply embedded in the flowers were pieces of the Ashion flower. As you know, once inhaled or ingested, its effects are deadly and irreversible. It shut down their organs, slowing their heartbeats in the blink of a star. We never had a chance of saving them."

A fresh surge of anger coursed through her. "Ashion is under strict lock and key in my realm. Only myself, General Lyric, and my magicians have the authority to access it. Everyone knows it is deadly to us. You want me to believe someone got past my staff—got past *me*—and hurt my daughters?! It's impossible! It can't be Ashion!"

"My Queen, we've run all of the necessary tests. Ashion was found in the princesses' blood. They were murdered."

"By whom?" she screamed. "Who would dare to hurt my babies?" She stopped abruptly.

Quickly, she jumped up and began running. "REVARIIIIIIIIII," she screamed. "REVARIIIIIIIIIIIIIIIIIIII!"

General Lyric sprang into action. "Vivacians! Grab your weapons now! Follow Queen Vivant to Rubarius!"

A ngela, a Revaltian soldier, rushed to find General Legend.

"General Legend!" she shouted.

General Legend rose from her desk. "What's the matter, Sgt. Angela?"

"The Vivacians! They're running across the Outer Realm to Rubarius!"

"What? Pull them up on the TranScreen."

"Yes, General Legend!"

Sure enough, hundreds of Vivacian soldiers were swiftly running towards Rubarius.

General Legend cocked her head and chuckled. "What in the universe is going on? Except for Queen Vivant, they know they can't enter the gates unless Queen Revari allows it."

"REVARRIIIIIIIIIIIIIIIIIII!!"

She moved closer to the TranScreen. *Was that Queen Vivant?*

Queen Revari was enjoying a wonderful, steamy bubble bath and listening to relaxing music when General Legend entered.

"Your Highness, Queen Vivant and her soldiers are outside our gates. She's screaming your name like a mad WomanForm. I've never seen her this unhinged."

She nibbled on a bit of velvety chocolate and sipped her expensive drink as if the general hadn't spoken. In awe of her blatant apathy amid the unfolding chaos, the general watched her lean back and stretch her legs until her polished red toes touched the end of the ruby tub.

"General Legend, this is the beginning of the end of Queen Vivant's reign." Queen Revari deeply and dramatically sniffed the air. "Do you smell that beautiful scent?"

"No. Smell what, My Queen?"

"Smells like three dead teen spirits!"

"She's scaling our wall!" exclaimed Private Jade. "Queen Vivant is scaling our wall!"

"I'LL KILL YOU REVARRRIIIIIIIIIIIIIII!"

"Is that Queen Vivant?" asked Sgt. Sheila in shock. In all her years under Queen Revari's reign, she'd never seen Queen Vivant so angry. Screaming threats was typical for Queen Revari.

But Queen Vivant? What in the universe could've enraged her to this level?

General Legend and Queen Revari were also watching Queen Vivant's antics from the steamy comfort of Queen Revari's bath chamber.

Her sister's tirade didn't move her. Not at all.

"Don't get in her way, Revaltians. I don't want any of your blood spilled on my gorgeous floors," she ordered as she poured more bath oil into the tub. "And make no mistake—in this state, she *will* kill you. Just let her come to me."

General Legend met her at the entrance of Rubarius's dining chamber. "I don't know why you're here, Queen Vivant, but you should watch your back. This isn't Platineous. You rule nothing in Rubarius!"

"You can either stand aside or I'll slit your throat right here. I'm not here to play with you."

"And I won't play with you either—" said General Legend.

"Let her in, General Legend," interrupted Queen Revari. "Queen Vivant, I'm about to have my supper. Be quick about why you've busted up my halls, then get out."

Quickly, General Legend moved aside. Queen Vivant rushed through the door and found Queen Revari sitting at a large dining table, slicing into a succulent cut of meat. The extravagant table, made of solid gold, was intricately adorned with diamonds and rubies. It was almost as impressive as the queen who sat at its head.

She savored the meat's smoky, buttery taste, groaning as it nearly melted in her mouth. She ate more than most MaleForms and had the muscle to prove it. White, hot anger coursed through Queen Vivant.

The LifeCelebration meal her daughters consumed hadn't had time to digest before they were murdered, yet here sat Queen Revari, celebrating her treachery.

"You're enjoying your last supper. I couldn't have asked for a better way to end you."

Queen Revari didn't take her attention off her meal. "Choose your words carefully, Queen Vivant. Any show of force against a ruler of Platirius—half or not—is treason. Since you were bold and dumb enough to break in here without your soldiers, I could order my Revaltians to mop you across my floors and toss you into my confinement chamber."

She cut into the meat again. "Locking you up is the second-best scenario other than shipping you off my planet." She sampled a small mass of mashed potatoes heaped with butter and roasted garlic.

"Your planet? You are not the only queen! Is that why you murdered my daughters? Hoping I'd leave with them when they're shipped into the sun?"

Queen Revari's head swiveled up.

She even moves like a snake, thought Queen Vivant.

"What in the galaxy are you talking about?" she bellowed. "I haven't killed anyone!" She perused her sister with a dark look. "Yet," she pointedly added.

She looked at her with a loathing she'd never realized she could feel. "I didn't expect you to be WomanForm enough to admit it, but it doesn't matter. Rise and take up your BrainStaff. Let's end this feud, Queen Revari."

"The only thing I'm going to take up is this fork and by the time it reaches my mouth, you'd better tell me what you're babbling about. Or I'll have you thrown out of here from the highest roof. I'm in no mood for your nonsense."

"Are you in the mood to die?"

Her eyes glowed red. "That's the last time you'll threaten me. I'll ask you once more. What do you want from me?"

Queen Vivant pointed her BrainStaff inches from her face. "Your head."

She threw her fork onto the plate.

Before she could rise, Queen Vivant threw a heavy dining chair against the wall and jumped on the table. She swung her BrainStaff, sending plates, glassware, and steaming hot, savory, and sweet dishes flying. Queen Revari screamed as a stream of hot soup splashed over her thighs.

"I'll kill you slowly!"

"No. I'm going to take my time killing *you*. You took away what was precious to me. You're nothing to me now."

"You. Crazy. *Whore*! I've told you I have *not* killed anyone! My nieces? Are you that daft you think I'd want to see my nieces dead? That's much less fun than seeing them burst into tears after I dethrone you and rule Platirius! That's your problem! You don't have any imagination!"

"And you no longer have any reason to live. Let's gooooooo, Queen Revari."

"Oh, Queen Vivant," she sneered. "You're not bad enough to end me!"

"General Legend!" she called, raising one hand in the air. "My BrainStaff!"

Her weapon was already in General Legend's hand. She tossed it to her queen, who caught it deftly.

Queen Revari's crimson gaze glowed menacingly at her. "You were saying?"

General Lyric burst into the dining chamber. "Queen Vivant! We have surveillance you should see!"

"Not now, General Lyric!" snapped Queen Vivant.

"But Queen Vivant!"

"I said not now!" she shouted. "I have business to settle." Looking Queen Revari in the eyes, she said, "I hope you missed

Father. You hated him in life. Maybe the two of you will get along in Hell!"

"Queen Vivant, Queen Revari didn't kill the princesses!" cried General Lyric.

Not taking her eyes off Queen Revari, she said, "You'd better start making sense. And fast."

Shaking her head slowly, General Lyric said, "One of our Vivacians just brought footage of the gardening chamber. We have the images of the intruder breaking in and obtaining the Ashion plant. It tracked all his movements from the moment he stole the Ashion flowers until—when he placed them in the princesses' LifeCelebration gift boxes. It wasn't Queen Revari."

"You should've pulled the footage long before she broke in here," said Queen Revari. "How were you selected to be a general? General Legend would never be so incompetent."

"Why would someone else hurt my daughters? No one hates me more than my sister."

"Please watch, My Queen," said General Lyric.

General Lyric moved to the TranScreen and inserted the thin, almost transparent disk. The WomenForms watched the intruder on the TranScreen.

"It's the Human!" exclaimed General Legend. She turned to General Lyric. "You allowed him to roam about Platineous freely?"

"Of course not!" said General Lyric.

"Silence," said both queens.

They watched as the Human male moved swiftly through the halls and into the gardening chamber. He cut three roses before pulling the soft bulbs of the Ashion flower from its stems and shoved them into his pockets.

He paused to look at the clock on the wall. Queen Vivant gasped when he pulled out a small package and unwrapped it. Inside was a dining staff uniform! Quickly, he donned it, covering his face with a mask.

He exited the gardening chamber and paused to be buzzed into the dining chamber. Once the door opened, he went to a table laden with sixteen gifts for each princess.

He opened the smallest boxes and found three exquisite diamond bracelets. Pocketing them, he pulled the roses from under his disguise and placed the bulbs of the Ashion plant inside each of them. Then he put the roses inside the boxes and rewrapped them.

To the untrained eye, the table was perfect. There was no sign anything had been tampered with. He knew precisely how to redecorate the gifts. Once finished, he quietly exited the dining chamber and entered the halls again. Then he looked directly into the camera and mouthed something.

"All of you will die," interpreted General Lyric.

Tears spilled from Queen Vivant's eyes.

Dry-eyed, hungry, and irritated, Queen Revari glared at her sister. "Wipe your face and get out of my palace," she said coldly. "You were stupid enough to allow a Human to roam your halls unsupervised. Then you broke in here and blamed me! And the universe thought you were competent enough to share Platirius with me? Ridiculous!"

"Queen Revari!" said General Lyric. "She just lost her daughters! Have you no heart?"

Queen Revari pinned her with an icy stare. "I have a stomach. And it's rumbling."

As they watched the footage, the dining staff cleaned up the mess Queen Vivant had made. The table was reset so she could dine.

Still staring at Queen Vivant, she said, "I won't hold my breath for an apology, nor do I need one." She sat down and began cutting into another expertly prepared, medium-well cut of meat. "I'll be over to Platineous after I finish my meal. I trust your staff will have more sense than you and allow me to see my nieces one last time."

"I'm sorry, Reve," whispered Queen Vivant.

"Save it, Vivant. Get out now." Her frosty, silver eyes flickered toward General Lyric. "Where is the Human now?"

"I don't report to you."

Her cold smile chilled the general. "It was *my* nieces who died, but you need *her* to ask *you* about their murderer at a time such as this? You're just as simple-minded as my sister. Get out. Both of you."

"Where is he?" asked Queen Vivant.

"He's asleep in Platineous's confinement chamber."

Queen Revari laughed. "Nothing like a murder to tire you out. That would've never happened on Rubarius. I don't allow

Humans to roam about my halls. I would've ordered for him to be held down under the laser scanner."

"We don't torture LifeForms on Platineous," said General Lyric.

She looked up from her plate at Queen Vivant. "I bet that's a mistake you won't repeat, isn't it?" She forked up another piece of meat.

"How can you eat after what's happened?" asked General Lyric.

"How could you let a finite Human kill three princesses under the watch of a queen and an entire army?" countered Queen Revari. "Never in my father's time or all the reigns of our ancestors has such incompetence shamed Platirius. You should resign, General. Today. And Vivant? Maybe you should send yourself into the sun with your daughters. You're not fit to lead the other half of Platirius."

General Lyric eyed her in disgust. "Your heart is colder than Space, Queen Revari. Had this Human not been caught in the act on the footage, I'd say you planned this. It would all work out for your good if Queen Vivant succumbed to her grief, wouldn't it?"

Exasperated, General Legend asked, "Don't you Vivacians get tired of blaming the innocent?"

Queen Revari narrowed her eyes. "You've never had sufficient brain cells, General Lyric. I want you to listen as closely as possible without getting confused. Had that Human been on Rubarius, I would've locked him down with searing lasers. He would've been in too much pain to even think of raising his mediocre hand to my nieces."

Her eyes slid to Queen Vivant. "Your queen does not share my acumen for punishing our enemies. This is precisely why three innocent Platirians have lost their lives today, and our planet is in mourning. Out of respect for my nieces, I command all Rubarian flags to be lowered to half stance."

General Legend nodded toward a couple of soldiers to carry out her order.

"Their deaths aren't on me," continued Queen Revari. "The fault lies with *you* and the queen you swore allegiance to. As the leader of the Vivacian army, you are most definitely to blame for slacking on defense."

Pointing a sharp knife at General Lyric, she said, "King Dubian would have never trusted outsiders with that amount of freedom. If you want someone to blame, find a mirror and make sure you and my sister are standing front and center. General Legend, get them out of my sight."

"Certainly, Queen Revari. This way, Queen Vivant and General Lyric," said General Legend.

Queen Revari forked up another piece of meat as they were led out of Rubarius. She was genuinely enjoying her meal. And why not? She'd certainly earned it. Her plan was working perfectly. She only wished there were four deaths on Platineous instead of three.

Queen Revari: 3. Queen Vivant: 0.

She's an incredible actress.

General Legend watched Queen Revari crying over the bodies of the young princesses. Once, she had witnessed her shed genuine tears, but that was another time. No one was surprised she hadn't cried at King Dubian's DeathCeremony.

Today, General Legend witnessed Queen Revari putting on the performance of her lifespan. The steady flow of tears she summoned were for herself. At first, she didn't know how she'd conjure emotion she didn't feel.

Yet, when she thought of how unfair it was to share Platirius with Queen Vivant after expertly killing King Dubian, she found it easy to cry hysterically.

Although she liked Princess Teenah, she loathed Queen Vivant's other daughters. In the end, she was collateral damage. She had been truthful when she informed Queen Vivant that she would have rather seen the princesses live miserably under her authority as Platirius's rightful leader.

Getting them out of the way was a solid plan. If Queen Vivant didn't take her own life, Queen Revari planned for her to be distracted from her duties until she succeeded in absorbing Earth into Platirius.

From what she understood of the Surveyors' long-winded summary, all she had to do was manipulate the Humans, causing them to wreak havoc in their lives. They were already good at doing that on their own, without provocation.

When enough of the world was in chaos, it would be easy to take control of Earth. Their leaders were already powerless against their weapons and crafts, yet none were required to win Earth. The best way to win against an enemy was to divide a house against itself.

Humans were skilled at warring against each other. However, when at war with themselves, they always lost. Unbeknownst to many of them, the mind was the most potent weapon they had. Once disarmed, she wouldn't need to kill them. They'd destroy themselves.

Platirians had a unique gift of taking complete control of Human minds, but they couldn't do it without free will. This was the most essential decree set by The One for Platirius's rulers to obey. To take Earth, Humans would have to choose to place themselves in peril.

She was confident they would. In return, she'd acquiesce to their selfish desires. Since it was considered more masculine to fight and shed blood with weapons, King Dubian and past MaleForm rulers had eschewed using the full potential of this power.

She knew better. Yes, it was quicker to kill with the BrainStaff and sword, but it wasn't as pleasurable as watching people suffer by their own hands. The Humans' unrelenting need for acceptance and to be admired would be their ultimate undoing. The power trip derived from having lesser Beings under her control was sheer *exhilaration*.

And? You didn't need to wash off blood at the end of the battle. MaleForms were too far too addlebrained to comprehend this. Yes—manipulating the Humans was crucial to her success. Her plan would surely fail if Queen Vivant intervened. Then the Humans would go back to living their pathetic lives, unscathed.

So, the only way to stop her from caring about the plight of Humans was to direct her focus elsewhere. What was better than grief to make a MotherForm give up on her duty? It was almost too perfect.

After wiping away the last of her selfish tears, she surmised that without having Queen Vivant on her back, taking Earth would be more fun than she'd had in quite a while.

The DeathCeremony of Platineous's fallen heirs was more lavish than anyone of their time had seen. Three beautifully decorated death crafts held the royal daughters. They wore splendid silver gowns with crowns of roses laced with diamonds adorning their heads.

Heavy diamond necklaces, bracelets, and diamond-encrusted shoes complemented the look. They looked as if they were going to a ball. To Queen Vivant's dismay, there would be no more celebrations in their future.

Their grief-stricken mother was sending them off to their final glory to be welcomed by searing rays in the heart of the sun. She contemplated joining her daughters as she stood with them in the Outer Realm.

And why not? There was nothing left for her now. No parents. No husband. And now—tears burst and flowed from her eyes as she cried out into the darkness of Space. She wailed in anguish, questioning the will of The One. What had she done to displease Him that He would take those most precious to her?

Despite her grief, the celebration had been well executed. Since the death of King Dubian, billions of Platineons and Rubarians stood side by side as a single unit of Platirius for the sendoff of their princesses. The attendees noted Queen Revari hadn't left her sister's side since the initial preparations began.

It was the first time Rubarius stood with Platineous. The Vivacian and Revaltian armies flanked on opposite sides of the Outer Realm. Each soldier held the flags of Platineous and Rubarius in an elaborate show of unity. Nameless, faceless Platirians spoke of their love for the fallen, young royal WomenForms.

Far too deep in the fog of despair, Queen Vivant hadn't seen or heard them. By the end of the DeathCeremony, one speech stood out. All eyes were on Queen Revari as she ascended platinum stairs and placed herself in the center of Platineous's death chamber.

"I wish I weren't here today. I wish this hadn't happened but it did. This was a senseless act committed by one who never belonged here. He should've been shipped back to his planet the moment he set foot on our grounds. A venomous Human dared to challenge who we are as a planet. As a race. We are Platirians. We have existed for millions of years. We've fought countless wars and brought down inferior populations. We are the exception to the rule concerning excellence and superiority."

She looked around at the crowd, determined to make it seem as if she was just as heartbroken as them.

"I stand before you, not as the queen of Rubarius. I am here as the loving aunt of Princess Teenah, Princess Tarah, and Princess Tyre, the rightful heirs to the throne of Platineous. Our bloodline would have continued through these three beautiful young WomenForms. Now they've been cut down in the prime of their lives. Sixteen summers is much too young to die!"

Someone gasped in the audience when a WomanForm fainted.

Irritated by the interruption, she pointed a slender finger at her. "Get that WomanForm out of here," she ordered before returning to the attendees.

She carefully crafted her expression into dark melancholy, belying suppressed elation. She thoroughly enjoyed being the center of attention.

"See how our grief overwhelms us? Not only has he destroyed the lives of three impressionable future queens. He has ruined the lives of their mother, Queen Vivant, and myself. And?

He has desecrated our home. His wicked actions have made you forget the peace and stability my sister and I have worked tirelessly to provide for you."

She raised her hands high in the air, commanding their attention. "Hear me, Platirians! We were robbed of their grace and beauty. No more will we see their smiles or hear their laughter. Most importantly, our queendoms—our entire planet is affected by his cruelty."

She paused and looked into the eyes of Queen Vivant. "Our successors are *dead*. They are never coming back," she said with a searing ring of finality. She smiled inwardly as uncontrolled sobs wracked Queen Vivant's tall form.

"So where does that leave us? Unlike my sister, I was never blessed with ChildForms. Without proper successors to lead, Platineous and Rubarius will fall when Queen Vivant and I die. We cannot allow this to happen. Severe punishment mustn't stop with the Human. It should extend to Earth as well."

Chapter 4

"If we allow a Human to get away with what he's done, how many more will come to Platirius trying to destroy us? Forgiveness is a skill my sister knows well, but this is no time to demonstrate forbearance. How many nations in the galaxy will regard that as a show of weakness?"

General Lyric looked around at the mourners. She felt their energy shift as they listened intently to Queen Revari. She knew exactly what she was doing. If she and the Revaltians attacked Earth, she'd have their support. No one would oppose her.

But would Queen Vivant?

"Platirians have never been weak, and we aren't going to begin now. We must make an example of this Human in front of all the galaxy's armies. He must stand trial and be sentenced to execution. Not a quick death, mind you. His punishment must be slow and torturous. On this dreadful day, I humbly ask for your allegiance to the thrones of Queen Vivant and myself. Let us stand together and rid our planet of this vile, disgusting Human and never be open to any treaties of peace in the future with Earth. Are you with us?"

Several calls of agreement rang out in the crowd. Sheer ecstasy coursed through her body as their chants for vengeance became louder.

"Louder!" she shouted. "Death to the Humans! Death to the Humans!"

"Death to the Humans! Death to the Humans!" chanted the crowd. She descended the stairs as rounds of yelling and clapping surrounded her.

General Lyric scanned the parameter again before centering on Queen Revari. She hadn't bought her show of grief for a moment. She had a nagging suspicion she was behind the deaths of Queen Vivant's daughters. Queen Revari had wanted to conquer Earth for a long time. Now she had the support of the Platirians.

The deaths of the princesses had placed her not only by Queen Vivant's side, but all Platirians were now regarding her in a new light. Whether they realized it or not, she had just positioned herself as the more decisive leader of the two realms.

Queen Vivant's tragedy was working to Queen Revari's advantage. No one had more to gain from the princesses' deaths than her. General Lyric wondered how she would prove it.

As she watched the queens hug, a cold feeling of dread swept upon her. They must not be taken in by her illusions. General Lyric knew she *hated* her sister. Tears flowed from Queen Revari's eyes, then opened suddenly and rested on her. Glowing a fiery red and brimming with venom, they bore into her with a hatred she felt deep in her soul.

She met her gaze steadily. She knew Queen Revari was aware she was on to her. That made her the number one threat to the Revaltians and their queen. But she wouldn't back down. She had never feared her and wouldn't start now.

She knew Queen Vivant better than anyone. She was kind and fair, but she'd lost the only true family she had left. She'd been there to comfort her through the losses of King Dubian and her husband, General Kron.

This time, it was different. The wounds in Queen Vivant's heart had been cut far too deep. Grief over losing her ChildForms surpassed any former tragedies she'd suffered.

She would take out her anger and sorrow on the Human. This was precisely what Queen Revari wanted to happen. Without proof the Human didn't act alone, she couldn't share what she suspected. Not yet. She hoped she could expose her before it was too late.

Queen Vivant watched the sendoff of her daughters into the sun through blurred vision. She wanted to turn the small crafts around and keep her babies with her forever. In her heart, she knew it wasn't possible.

As the crafts sped away until they were no longer in sight, blind rage erupted within her. If she had her way, the Human would already be burning. She looked forward to seeing him tossed into the unrelenting Flames of Justice.

As the last dishes of the DeathCeremony feast were cleared away, Queen Revari sighed inwardly. Between listening to hours of Queen Vivant's incessant wailing and idiotic talk of how enduring and loved the princesses were, she thought she'd vomit. The DeathCeremony had taken longer than she'd expected. Now, she was ready to get on with her plans.

In the nick of time, she resisted the urge to drive her nails into Queen Vivant's skin. Gently, she squeezed her sister's hand, giving false reassurance. Turning to her, she said, "Vivi, I know we've been at odds for quite a while."

General Lyric's head snapped up at the sound of 'Vivi.' Queen Revari hadn't called Queen Vivant that since they were very young. When Platirius split into two realms, she'd forbidden Queen Vivant from referring to her as 'Reve.' General Lyric thought becoming Rubarius's queen had only exacerbated her narcissistic tendencies.

At King Dubian's DeathCeremony, the Rubarians and the Platineons had stood on opposite sides within the death chamber. It was a blatant show of discordance from Queen Revari, clearly angered she hadn't been appointed the sole queen of Platirius.

For General Lyric, that was suspicious as well. For years, she'd believed Queen Revari was responsible for King Dubian's death. Once his reign ended, she hadn't wanted to connect with Queen Vivant on any level.

So why now? Surely it wasn't due to the deaths of the princesses. She hated them all, even Princess Teenah, although she pretended to be her friend. Queen Revari was very good at lying and faking emotions she didn't possess. She was confident she was up to something.

Queen Revari ignored General Lyric's accusatory stare. The insolent whore. She was chomping at the bit to kill her. Slowly. Almost as slowly as she wanted to kill the Human.

"Allow me to take the Human off of your hands. We'll give him the proper agony he deserves right before he sees death."

General Lyric also turned to Queen Vivant. "My Queen, the laws of the galaxy decree that the Human should face trial before all of Platineous. The public would never forgive us if we denied them the right to hear the evidence and see the Human justly punished."

Queen Revari raised an eyebrow. She had to admit, even she hadn't known if she could pull off murdering three royal ChildForms. Nevertheless, removing them was a matter of necessity.

Sharing the throne with Queen Vivant was terrible enough. Unless murdered, the life cycles of Platirians were a thousand years to the average lifespan of ninety-nine Human years.

Time on Platirius was not counted as Humans counted time on Earth. Also, ascension to the throne was through birthright.

King Dubian hadn't minded when Queen Revari chose to be a warrior over a wife. Ironically, it was the only choice he'd permitted her to have. In another time, Fate decided she would never become a MotherForm.

While she didn't hold teenage WomenForms in high regard, she genuinely loved younger ChildForms. Yet, she couldn't extend that love to her nieces. They were the spawns of Queen

Vivant and General Kron, whom she had despised almost as much as her sister.

Princess Tyre was correct in her assessment of her aunt. Queen Revari had never spent time with them or bothered to comfort them when they were babies. She seldom acknowledged their presence unless she had something to gain. Even then, she had only interacted with Princess Teenah, the jolliest of the trio.

She thought Princess Tyre and Princess Tarah were too spoiled and selfish. Entitled. She couldn't stand the blood in their veins. Blood that now lay black and curdled in their cold corpses thanks to the incredible power of the Ashion flower.

Before the princesses died, she had infiltrated some of her gardening staff into Platineous's gardening chamber to study Ashion's effects and report back to her.

Although Ashion was deadly to Platirians, its potency would not kill Humans. Once inhaled or ingested, the Humans she'd experimented on only became highly addicted. In addition to ravenous hunger, she discovered Ashion made them delusional and easy to control.

Besides King Dubian, no other ruler had dared to interfere with Earth. When Queen Revari became aware of her father's plans to claim it, it sped up her plans to get rid of him. There was no way she'd allow him to become invincible.

That right belonged to *her*. She'd worked too hard for too long to finally be in a position to ascend to the throne. If General Lyric thought she would get in her way, she had best think again.

"These are different circumstances," Queen Revari said evenly. "No royal ChildForms have ever been murdered on Platirius." She slightly emphasized *murdered* and was pleased when Queen Vivant winced.

"I'm quite sure all Platirians would understand if we didn't abide by the rules for this very delicate matter. Vivi, I wasn't there for the princesses as I should have been. This is my chance to make it up to them and avenge their deaths," she said, watching Queen Vivant's face closely.

For a moment, Queen Vivant was silent. She wanted nothing more than to see the Human die by her hand. She'd had more than enough time to mull it over, but the decision to deny the Human a trial wasn't solely up to her or Queen Revari.

The justice council decided what was legal and just. That meant Platineous and Rubarius, as two halves of Platirius, were bound by its laws and policies. It was a form of checks and balances to ensure the rulers abided by the galaxy's laws.

It had almost been abolished during King Dubian's reign. Once he acquired Coldarius, he sought to dismantle the council but was prevented by a vote from Queen Opal.

Queen Opal had been a member of the council on Coldarius and fully believed in its duty to govern the laws. It was the only time she had disagreed with her husband.

King Dubian had been surprised, but didn't challenge her vote. As such, the justice council still stood. However, after she acquired Earth, in laying down the foundation of her new empire, she'd dismantle the council.

"Let's go to the Chief Counselor," said Queen Vivant. It couldn't hurt to ask. Maybe Queen Revari was right. The murders of royal ChildForms were unheard of throughout the entire galaxy. Surely, the council would side with her wishes.

Queen Revari didn't share her sister's sentiments. The council was an immovable force in adhering to the laws. However, she had a role to play, and she'd play it to the very end. The end of the justice council and Platineous.

C hief Counselor Adoni listened intently as the queens laid out their intentions for what was to become of the Human. She nodded to General Lyric and General Legend in greeting and shook her head slowly.

Like every Platirian, she was saddened by the loss of Princess Teenah, Princess Tarah, and Princess Tyre. Their deaths had rocked both sides of Platirius to its core.

She felt for Queen Vivant's plight and agreed with her assessment—such an atrocious event had never transpired in Platirius's history. Nevertheless, she must consult galaxy law before the council made a decision.

She adjusted her glasses and waved one hand in the air. In an instant, thousands of legal vernaculars hovered over them. Closing her fist, she pulled the excerpt she wanted, amplifying it for all to see.

"According to galaxy law, any outsider who kills a Platirian must have a trial before execution. The Human has no rights on Platirius. A trial is not for the benefit of proving his guilt or innocence. It is for all Platirians to hear what he has done and for the actions to be recorded in the Eternal Hall of Records. He will be executed regardless, for we have no responsibility to legally represent lower LifeForms from other planets."

Removing her glasses, she rubbed her tired eyes before replacing them. None of them had been able to sleep well since the tragedy.

"What's most insulting is he came from planet Earth. It possesses the lowest levels of intellect in the entire galaxy. Humans are fatuous Beings who are easily fooled by their cretinous technology and dilettantish ones who betray their governments. This particular law has stood for millions of years, and it is just. I am in full agreement with it."

She paused to peruse the WomenForms before continuing. "The Human must not be transferred to Rubarius to be tortured before death. He will remain on Platineous and face trial. Afterward, he will be immediately executed by being burned alive within the unquenchable Flames of Justice."

Her sharp gaze assessed the laws, ensuring she interpreted them exactly as they were written before turning to regard Queen Vivant.

"You have been an amazing ruler of Platineous. You are honorable and earned my respect many years ago. There is no request you could make that I wouldn't grant. I'm sorry, but this is something I cannot do. It is above the scope of my duties as Chief Counselor."

Her eyes brushed the brain-shaped gavel on her desk before refocusing on Queen Vivant. "Do not fret, My Queen. The Flames of Justice are not akin to fire made on Earth. He will not experience what Humans perceive to be a normal death. There will be no ascension into the afterlife to receive judgment by The One. His torment will be the excruciating pain of the flames licking at his flesh for eternity."

It was the first time that the queens learned how the Flames of Justice worked. Since their reigns, no one had been arrested on either side of Platirius. Ultimately, they both agreed this was the best punishment for the Human.

Queen Vivant was satisfied that there would be no end to his suffering. "I thank you, Chief Counselor Adoni," she said.

She nodded. "You're welcome, Queen Vivant. I wish I could do more to help. The trial begins tomorrow after sunrise. The council will be ready to hear the case and witness the criminal's descension into eternal execution. My heart is with you during this difficult time."

She observed Queen Revari for a long moment before she spoke again. "Although we cannot change how the Human will be punished, I must question if there will be any show of force against Earth from the Revaltians."

Queen Vivant's dejected expression motivated her to choose her words carefully. "You have experienced what no MotherForm should. However, suppose a war is launched on

Earth by the Revaltians. In that case, you must weigh the consequences of turning your back on the duty bestowed to you by The One, or having an amicable relationship with Queen Revari."

Keeping her face free of emotion, Queen Revari stared at the Chief Counselor as she continued.

"I will caution you—The One is not an enemy you want to have. He is more powerful than any Being in the galaxy but is not a Being. He is *above* all Beings. He made all of us and assigned us to different regions of space to live under His Authority. No one, not even your precious daughters, must be more important than Him."

She glanced sideways at Queen Revari. "I don't expect Queen Revari to care one bit about His expectations. I'm afraid you have many tough decisions to make regarding this matter."

Queen Vivant was silent, her mind still focused on punishing the Human. She'd barely heard what she'd said. On the other hand, Queen Revari had listened to every word.

However, she didn't feel the need to address her. She knew how Queen Vivant operated and had already set in motion how she'd get her out of the way.

No worries, she thought. But—someone better find the Chief Counselor a chair for the show she'd prepared. And a comfortable one. To Queen Revari, Chief Counselor Adoni was as imbecilic as an eight-legged space dog.

Still, she was right about one thing—Queen Revari didn't care about The One's wishes. She intended to bring Earth to its knees. And no one—not even He—would stop her.

The morning of the Human's trial began with gray, gloomy skies. Sharp, biting rain poured down on solemn Platirians as they entered the justice chamber. Chief Counselor Adoni scanned the room.

Surprised, she noted Queen Vivant wasn't in attendance. Still, it was her duty to have the trial begin on time. She rapped her BrainGavel sharply on the table.

"All will come to order!" she called soundly. "In the case of Platineous vs. Kyle Kaufmann, the defendant will rise."

Pointedly, she regarded the Human and said, "Kyle Kaufmann, you are hereby charged with the murders of Princess Teenah, Princess Tarah, and Princess Tyre of the Platineous empire. You have also been charged with stealing multiple Ashion plants and trespassing on our planet. How do you plead?"

"I plead not guilty, Chief Counselor," stated Kyle. "I didn't murder anyone!"

Murmurs of displeasure rose within the crowd. Kyle felt the intensity of their hatred, but there was nothing he could do.

They thought he'd killed Queen Vivant's daughters. They had come to watch him die.

"That's enough," she said. "I asked what you plead. I didn't ask you to elaborate."

She called for silence in the court before addressing him again. "Understand this. You are not here to defend yourself. Our laws do not work like the ones on your planet. This trial is for both queendoms of Platineous and Rubarius to hear what you have done. Afterward, the record will be sealed, and you will spend eternity burning in the Flames of Justice."

Kyle bowed his head. "I don't understand how I can be set up for something I didn't do."

"Our ways are not for you to understand," she said coldly.

Tilting her head to the left, she said, "You Humans are so cocky. So full of yourselves you believe the entire universe views you as equals. It doesn't. Today, we will make an example of you."

Her raven-black eyes narrowed. "And for your sake, I hope Queen Revari doesn't annihilate Earth. As pathetic as your race is, it would be a shame for all of your kind to suffer due to the sheer arrogance of one lowly Human."

"Why do you hate us?" asked Kyle.

"You dare ask such a question? After what you've done?"

"I didn't—"

"Be quiet! I'll hear no more of your buffoonery!" She nodded to a Vivacian soldier. "Silence him."

The soldier wrapped a band of heavy chrome tape was wrapped around his mouth and violently shoved him into the chair. He sat at a solitary table in the middle of the justice chamber.

The Chief Counselor sat on a high podium with three Justice Counselors on her right and left sides. In all, seven Justice Counselors would observe and record the evidence presented before sentencing him.

Three witnesses were called to testify against him. He wouldn't be allowed even to defend himself. Kyle wondered what he'd done to deserve such a fate. He also wondered if it was all a dream.

Aliens? Putting him on trial? It was ridiculous! It had to be a dream he'd wake up from soon. They certainly didn't look like any Aliens he'd seen in movies or comic books. All of them were beautiful women. Even the stern Chief Counselor. It was impossible to determine how old they were. If they had ages.

But what did it matter? He'd never have another birthday all because of some crazy Alien woman's thirst for power. He wanted to explain what happened to him, but he wasn't sure how. The truth belied all laws of science. Worst of all, the Platirians had refused to hear his side of the story.

Chief Counselor Adoni nodded to the entrance of the justice chamber. "Now we'll hear the first witness."

Adeline Aikos was the first witness. She nervously stood before the justice council, her hands slightly trembling. She had never been summoned to the justice chamber. No one since King Dubian's time had been. No one had wanted to be.

He'd been a ruthless leader. No one in Old Platirius, as the locals called it, had dared to cross him. Now, here she stood, ready to testify to what she'd seen. She was more than ready to send the Human to his death.

"Ms. Aikos, please take a seat. You will now explain to us what you witnessed."

"I was gathering vegetables for the dining chamber staff to prepare for the princesses' LifeCelebration. I looked up and saw a Human walking to the entrance of the gardening chamber. I was shocked. We haven't seen Humans here since King Dubian was alive. Even then, I'd never seen any walking around freely." She paused, wringing her hands.

"Go on," urged a Justice Counselor.

"I expected him to be denied entry, but he waved his hand over the TeleShield and was buzzed in! Just as if he was a Platirian, born and raised here! I couldn't believe it! So, I followed him. And I saw—"

"Yes?"

"I saw him cut three roses before going to the Ashion plant and cutting off a lot of the bulbs. Then he put the bulbs in his pockets and left." She looked up at the Justice Counselors. "That's all I saw."

"Did you tell anyone what you saw, Ms. Aikos?"

Adeline trembled. "No, I didn't."

"Why?"

"I—I figured if he was walking around Platineous, someone must have given him permission—"

81

"Give a *Human* permission to roam our planet, granting him access to a plant that is deadly to Platirians?" asked another Justice Counselor incredulously. "WomanForm, are you daft? Who in their right mind would allow a Human to do such a thing?! The very idea is unfathomable! Why didn't you alert the Vivacian soldiers about this?"

Adeline bowed her head in shame. "It wasn't my place to say anything!" she cried. "I'm just garden staff! Who am I to report anything to the Vivacians? They are the authority on Platineous. It's their responsibility to know what goes on and protect us!"

"So, you feel you're exempt from preventing a catastrophe from occurring? Are you saying it wasn't your duty to save the princesses?"

"Enough!" said the Chief Counselor. "Ms. Aikos is a law-abiding Platirian. She didn't kill three royal Platirians. A Human did."

She pointed to Kyle. "Ms. Aikos, was this the Human you saw?"

Adeline looked at Kyle and nodded. "Yes, Chief Counselor! It was he who stole the Ashion plant! I saw him with my own eyes."

"Ms. Aikos is correct," said Chief Counselor Adoni. "It is the duty of the Vivacian army, specifically the Surveillance team, to monitor and keep order on this planet. Not ordinary Platirians. And with that, we'll call our next witness. General Lyric of the Vivacian army, come forth!" She turned to Adeline. "You are excused, Ms. Aikos."

"Yes, Chief Counselor," said Adeline, hurriedly leaving the justice chamber.

Standing lean and tall, General Lyric entered the justice chamber. Raising her right hand, she stood before the Justice Counselors and swore to be truthful before taking the seat Adeline Aikos had left.

"General Lyric, you have served under Queen Vivant for many years. Your leadership of the Vivacians has been impressive—until now. Are you able to tell us how this Human got past your soldiers and went undetected into the gardening chamber?"

"Chief Counselor, I saw the same footage as you. We have a surveillance team who monitors all movement on Platineous. They are the best at what they do. I questioned them extensively and they reported that he didn't show up on our monitors when he entered the gardening chamber."

"How can that be when we have footage of him entering the gardening and the dining chambers?"

"I wish I knew," said General Lyric. "The footage we have is clear as the stars. As far as our surveillance shows, he didn't enter those chambers at any time on the day of the princesses' LifeCelebration." General Lyric pinned Kyle with a cold stare. "If we had seen him, he'd be dead right now. We must protect the royal family of Platineous. But we could not protect them from something we didn't see."

She sighed. "I would say the footage you have of his is false except—"

"Except the princesses are dead," finished the Chief Counselor. "That is a fact. This Human stole Ashion and placed it inside the princesses' gift boxes. We also found the jewelry he stole—the real presents he switched for the Ashion on him. The footage doesn't lie. Perhaps the error is on your part, General Lyric. Would it be fair to suggest your surveillance team was incompetent?"

"Impossible!" said General Lyric. "We have an impeccable record! We have never failed Platineous—"

"Until now," interrupted a Justice Counselor. "General Lyric, there's not enough room in this justice chamber to hold your enormous ego! We won't sit here and listen to how great your Vivacian army is when *three* princesses are dead! On *your* watch. It doesn't matter what your record was before. A lowly *Human* was allowed to roam our planet unsupervised. According to your testimony, he wasn't *seen*."

She pointed at Kyle. "This Human has no powers. How could he disguise himself from your devices? That tells me your soldiers weren't properly attending to their posts! Either they were asleep or straddling Simonius—oh yes, we're aware that at least one of your soldiers has been misbehaving with him! What we are one hundred percent certain of is they were *not* watching the Human closely. It is clear the Vivacians allowed this to happen."

At this, General Lyric jumped out of the seat. "That's absurd! We are loyal to Queen Vivant! We would never go against her. Unlike Queen Revari, we have no reason to hate her. She's been good to us and she's a fair queen."

Another Justice Counselor shook her head. "What does Queen Revari have to do with this?"

"Queen Revari hates Queen Vivant. She always has. Is it so farfetched to imagine she made this Human kill the princesses?" asked General Lyric. "She's the only one to benefit from all of this!"

"Yes, General Lyric. I think that's all it is—your imagination. Did you forget the Rubarians do not defend Platineous? They aren't even allowed on our grounds without Queen Vivant's permission. Not one device detected any trace of them or Queen Revari. She's never attended any celebratory events here and didn't yesterday. Do you have any proof to contradict what I just said?"

General Lyric sighed. "I don't yet. However—"

"There is no, 'however.' In all of the years I've witnessed generals born and die on Platirius, none of them have ever attempted to shirk their duty—"

"That's not what I'm doing—"

"—or shift the blame on someone else!" finished the Justice Counselor. "It is disgraceful you are refusing to take accountability for the utter failure of the army you lead! Yes, this Human killed the princesses. That wouldn't have happened had you been on top of your game! We're going to punish this Human. Today. No doubt about that!"

She peered over the high bench at General Lyric. "You and the Vivacians are not without fault here! This council doesn't have the power to strip you of your duties. As the ruler of

Platineous, only Queen Vivant has that right. If I were her, I'd not only strip you of your title, I'd banish you from Platineous! You allowed this Human to do what he did. Therefore, you are equally responsible for the deaths of the princesses. You're not fit to be General of the Vivacians. Not on this day. Nor any."

Every Vivacian in attendance bowed their heads. They didn't agree with everything the Justice Counselor said, but they had failed Queen Vivant in not stopping the Human. For that? They had no reasonable excuse. Now the credibility of their general was being shredded to pieces for all to see. It wasn't fair. She was right—they couldn't fight an unseen enemy.

She tried not to panic at the justice counselor's words. Queen Revari would have more of an advantage if she were removed as general. The Vivacians were a strong unit. Nevertheless, none of the soldiers under her could go up against General Legend and the Revaltians and win. Queen Revari was much too powerful.

What would Queen Vivant do? Would she take the Justice Counselor's advice and banish her from Platineous? Where would she go? Surely not to Rubarius? Without Queen Vivant's help, Queen Revari would have her shipped away to an unknown planet. She didn't want to think about the consequences surrounding that.

"General Lyric, you are excused," said the Chief Counselor.

She stood and bowed before the council. "It is my honor to serve Platineous."

Every Vivacian soldier saluted their general as she walked down the long corridor before falling in perfect succession behind her. One by one, the Vivacians left the justice chamber with spirits heavier than they'd ever felt. No one knew what Queen Vivant would do. They'd have to wait and see.

"We have one more witness to call. Nadia Bexly, come forth!"

As Ms. Bexly took her seat, the Chief Counselor said, "Ms. Bexly, you were scheduled to work in the dining chamber. Tell us what you saw on the afternoon of the princesses' deaths."

Nadia hesitated for only a moment. If she told the council what she saw, they'd think she was crazy and lock her up in the Chamber of Despair. She'd already been locked away there twice. She wasn't going back.

"I saw the Human enter the dining chamber and go to the gift table. He stole the jewelry from the boxes and replaced them with something I couldn't see. Whatever it was, it came from his pockets. Then he placed the bracelets in his pockets and left."

"Is there anything else?"

Nadia looked into the Chief Counselor's eyes. "No, Chief Counselor. There's nothing else."

"Very well then. You are free to go."

"Thank you, Chief Counselor."

Chief Counselor Adoni looked into the crowd and announced, "Platirians, the testimony you have heard today is now recorded and will be chronicled in Platineous's Hall of Records. Although many factors aided the Human in this unwarranted, unforgivable act, he was the only one on trial today. And now—he'll be sentenced accordingly."

She looked down at Kyle. "Kyle Kaufmann, you will now rise and face this council."

Shakily, he stood up and looked up at the council. Seven pairs of stone-cold eyes bore into his.

"You have been found guilty of theft and murder. You are hereby sentenced to death in the Flames of Justice, where you will burn for all of eternity. You will not die in the sense you know. For every second that passes, you will feel nothing except torturous pain."

She nodded to the justice guards. "Take him away."

Muffled, he tried to scream, but it was no use. He continued to scream as they led him out of the justice chamber, across the platinum sands of Platineous, through tall platinum grass to an open field of fire. He gasped.

The flames were intertwined with smoky blue, white, and platinum rays. It was the most beautiful thing he'd ever seen. Ironically, it was also the last thing his senses would experience. He held his breath as the guards tossed him into the flames.

At first, he felt nothing. Then, as the mysterious flames consumed his body, he felt pain he never imagined existed. The fire burned from *inside* his body. He felt his insides melting as he smelled scorching flesh.

Lifting his hands, he saw his skin was still intact, but the *feeling*. Oh God, the *agony* of the eternal fire as it charged through him. Liquid hot. Unbearable. He screamed and screamed.

Keeping her word, she telepathically uncovered the barriers inside Kyle's mind, allowing him to finally remember how he came to their planet. When his horrific cries swirled through Platineous, over the Outer Realm, and into the dark red halls of Rubarius, Queen Revari smiled.

Chapter 5

"My Queen, I think we have a problem," said Cyen.

"What is it?"

"One of the Platineons saw my powers shift. She saw me inside of the Human's shell."

Queen Revari continued staring out of the window at Earth. "Then you know what you must do, don't you?"

"I can't get inside Platineous without a host," said Cyen miserably.

She turned from the window. She needed a drink to hear the rest. Cyen waited as she poured a glass of wine.

"Who is she?"

"Her name is Nadia Bexley. She works in the dining chamber. Her mind is very unstable. She was locked away in the Chamber of Despair on two occasions."

Queen Revari laughed. "What on Platirius for?"

"She was passed up for a promotion. Twice. So she mentally disintegrated."

Queen Revari shook her head. On Platirius, competition played a considerable role in societal status. Even in King Anemi's reign, you were either of high status or no one.

"Why do you believe she saw you shift?"

"She was putting food on the tables when I switched the jewelry with the Ashion. I didn't expect anyone to be there. I shifted only for a moment. But when her eyes got big, I knew she saw me working through him."

"Then I'll have to take care of her," said Queen Revari quietly. She poured another glass of wine and handed it to Cyen. "Did anyone else see you?"

Cyen accepted the glass from her. "No, My Queen."

She slowly sipped the wine. "What about the surveillance? Did it catch you?"

Cyen shook her head. "No. Cia's spell is impenetrable. It was cast before I cast mine. My shifting didn't affect her magic."

"Good. We can't afford any mishaps. We've come too far now. We left some of our best dishes for the DeathCelebration on Platineous. Call for her to bring them back to Rubarius's dining chamber. Then—I'll have a little chat with Ms. Bexly."

Nadia trembled as the queen stared her down. What had she done? She hadn't told anyone she saw the Revaltian magician inside the Human. Who would believe her? Queen

Revari displayed a dazzling smile, quietly disarming Nadia. She used her beauty to her advantage when it benefited her.

"Have a seat Ms. Bexly. Thank you so much for bringing back my dishes."

"Of course, Queen Revari. Anything I can do to help," said Nadia nervously.

She poured a hot drink and served it to her. "Ms. Bexly, it is a tragic time. I hope you don't mind that I require your assistance," she said smoothly.

Nadia was surprised when she sat down too. It was rare for commoners to sit with royals. Overwhelmed by her beauty and impeccable manners, she asked, "What may I assist you with, My Queen?"

Her smile widened. "My Queen? Oh, I like that! You mustn't allow Queen Vivant to hear you say that. You're one of hers. She'd think you were being treasonous by showing me respect."

She was lying, of course, but Nadia didn't know that. Although saluting the queens on opposite sides of Platirius was frowned upon by both sides, it wasn't an act of treason.

"I'm sorry," whispered Nadia.

"No need for that! I won't tell my sister. But—" She paused long enough for Nadia to meet her eyes. "—I'm more concerned with what *you* may say, Ms. Bexly. You've spent some time in the Chamber of Despair. I've read your records. You seem to have an issue with hallucinations."

Nadia winced.

"This is a very delicate time for my sister. It wouldn't do for her to hear the incessant ramblings of an unstable WomanForm telling lies about one of my magicians."

She scanned Nadia's racing thoughts, keeping her smile hidden. "We were nowhere near Platineous when the princesses died. Wouldn't you agree?"

Nadia gasped. "I tend to see things that aren't there, Queen Revari."

Uncrossing her legs, Queen Revari stood and took the cup from her hands. "I know. And I'm going to help you with your little problem."

Nadia sucked in her breath. "You will? You'll cure me?"

Queen Revari looked into her eyes. "Of course. That's what rulers are for."

Before she could blink, they were standing in a room she'd never seen before. Dropping Queen Revari's hand, she looked around wildly. "Where are we?"

"We're on Earth," said Queen Revari. "In the year 1910." She circled a small, hard bed made of steel. Unsightly stained sheets covered a thin mattress. "This is called an asylum for lunatics." She placed a red-booted foot on the bed and said, "And here is where you'll stay."

"What's a lunatic?" asked Nadia.

"You. You are a lunatic and this is the perfect place for you. Just imagine what the Humans will do to you when you tell them you were born on another planet." Her cruel laugh made Nadia uneasy. "No one will believe you. If there's one thing Humans are good at, it's torture."

She looked around the small, cluttered room in satisfaction. "This is what you've earned for poking your nose into my affairs. I can't kill you without Queen Vivant finding out. But now that she's preoccupied with losing her brats, she's not keeping tabs on what I do. Which is precisely how I planned it to be."

She backed away as Queen Revari approached her. "I've worked hard all of my life for this moment. Do you think I will allow a mere dining staff to blow my plan out of Space? I've always believed torture is much more fun than killing. Cruelty is one of the few things Humans do best. Even though you're not one of them—hey! They don't know that!"

She moved Nadia backward until her legs touched the cool metal of the bed railing. "No one back home will track you, for no one knows you're gone. I've erased all memory of you from the minds of every Platirian except Queen Vivant. And she doesn't know you exist."

Thankfully, Queen Vivant hadn't attended the Human's trial. Otherwise, she wouldn't have been able to orchestrate Nadia's disappearance. "You have no family. No friends. So, no one misses you. Also, there's no record of your testimony against the Human either. Only the garden staff and General Lyric's testimonies are in Platineous's Hall of Records."

There was no point in trying to reason with her. Nadia had heard she was merciless, but she never thought she'd ever cross paths with her. She wished she hadn't been in the dining chamber that day.

"There are many things I control that your queen doesn't know about. After King Dubian died, I acquired a lot of power from a long-dead ruler I never knew. After he was killed, his power entered the Rubarius's grounds."

Her beautiful smile held no warmth. "After all of my father's scheming and controlling ways, I received an inheritance he'd kill to have." She sighed. "Isn't it ironic?"

Terrified, Nadia watched her smile slowly disappear. Queen Vivant isn't able to read my mind, so she's unaware of what I can do. King Dubian's favorite acquired his knowledge and much of it is useless since her heart is just as soft as her brain! How sad for her, yes?"

Panic rose in Nadia when she realized what the queen intended to do.

"Goodbye, Ms. Bexly. Enjoy your stay. Unfortunately for you, this will be the vacation of a lifetime."

"Don't leave me here!" cried Nadia. "Just kill me! Please, Queen Revari. Take my life. I give it to you freely!"

"I know. That's what makes this moment so sweet. I'll hear you begging the Humans to kill you long before death comes to claim you. That's my idea of a good time. Aren't you having fun, Nadia?"

Laughing, she vanished as Nadia sank to her knees, crying out in the darkness.

Queen Revari sat in her meeting chamber enjoying a steaming hot cup of CocoBerry tea. She was proud of the lush gardens surrounding her empire. After acquiring Rubarius, she secretly learned plants that thrived on Rubarius didn't grow on Platineous.

Nor did Platineous's plants survive on Rubarius. It was a saving grace that Ashion couldn't be grown within her queendom. General Lazy Lyric would've had a bit of proof she and the Revaltians were behind the attack on Queen Vivant's ChildForms.

Once she tasted the richness of the first CocoBerry plants, out of spite, she decreed Rubarius and Platineous would not share vegetation and sustenance. She'd also ordered the staff in her gardening chamber to work with the research chamber staff.

Together, they changed the plants' molecular structure, providing medicinal powders and food only for the Platirians living on Rubarius.

She wanted her subjects to be strong and vital. She couldn't abide unhealthy Platirians. Queen Vivant thrived on coddling weaklings such as Ms. Bexley. However, Platirians with debilitating issues—be they physical or mental—weren't welcome in Queen Revari's queendom.

She was relieved when most of them went to Queen Vivant after Platirius split. Under her tutelage, her powders and remedies quickly healed those assigned to her.

Queen Vivant didn't believe in using substances to heal Platirians. Instead, she chose to utilize her powers of Healing. Queen Revari thought using such a gift on commoners was a waste of precious time. Perhaps this was why she was not given the power of Healing. Well, that suited her just fine.

Every substance used on Rubarius came from its rich, lustrous soil. King Dubian had accidentally given her the idea of using plant-based approaches to become stronger and extend lifespans. While watching the Humans on the TranScreen, he scoffed at their dependence on manufactured substances that only shortened their lives.

Queen Revari also believed in cultivating vegetation to make weapons for war. Some of the plants were natural hallucinogens. Others had calming effects. And some would drive Platirians to commit unspeakable acts.

The potency of the plants she possessed had ten thousand times the adverse impact on Humans. Through secret experimentations during and after King Dubian's reign, she learned which plants provided the most damage to Humans—and what healed them.

One medicinal advantage she discovered was Callidut. Only a small amount was required to lull Humans into a calm, amicable state. Combined with mind control techniques, it was flawless in producing mindless shells, ready to do her will.

To its credit, Callidut was the answer to many of the Humans' idiotic prayers. Merely three weeks after initial ingestion, it caused significant weight loss and provided a noticeable youthful appearance. Weight and youth were the main things most Humans—females and males—obsessed over.

It was all too easy to plant spies in governments worldwide. Corruption paved the way for obtaining approval for their best weapon against the Humans, Callidut. What worked in their favor was no physical side effects.

No constipation, depression, or irreparable damage to the body. Addiction was inevitable as Callidut introduced an insatiable craving for more.

Other than the change in their brain structure, which was undetectable to human technology, the Platirian substance would be all the rage to Humans. They'd clamor for Callidut, making her acquisition of Earth as simple as playing a board game.

While experimenting with drugs and mind conditioning wasn't new to Humans, they'd never experienced it on the level of Platirians.

Gallium, Rubarius's chief gardening staff, was a master of cultivating various plants. His gift of experimenting with exotic plants had kept him alive. MaleForms were scarce on Rubarius and Platineous.

Only three survived after King Dubian's death—Dr. Barrios, the chief royal physician (who had agreed to betray King Dubian in exchange for keeping his life), Simonius, an expert galactic scientist and mathematician, and Gallium.

To everyone's astonishment, the sisters agreed Platirius had no use for MaleForms. Regardless of age, the new queens had subsequently shipped them into the sun, alive, with King Dubian's corpse. Queen Revari was prepared for a revolt from the WomenForms, yet it was not to be.

Years of being dominated under the rule of MaleForms had caused deep-seated hatred to spring between the SexForms. There was no love or trust in MaleForms. In the end, the decision to banish most MaleForm life was applauded by most of the WomenForms. Not a single one advocated for them to remain on Platirius.

Most importantly, MaleForms were forbidden to rule Platirius. They were too greedy, cruel, and destructive. They relished in oppressing WomenForms. It would not be tolerated during the new reign. Coming from Queen Revari, this was utter hypocrisy, of course. Yet, at least she was a WomanForm.

Platirius held thirty billion LifeForms—fifteen billion each on Platineous and Rubarius. The new queens had declared there was no need for procreation. Or romantic love. They would live and work as fellow Platirians without the destructive distractions that caused misery to lesser Beings.

Gallium, Dr. Barrios, and Simonius had proven their worth and allegiance to the queens. If they had deep-seated sexual desires, they knew better than to let them be known. If either queen even imagined they wanted to prey on the WomenForms, they'd be thrown into the Flames of Justice. Immediately.

Now Gallium was being summoned to Queen Revari's palace. He wasn't worried. He knew he hadn't done anything to anger her. He was one of the few privy to her plans to conquer Earth.

Although he was a MaleForm, he was proud his queen needed the plants he'd designed and grown to be successful in her endeavor. He didn't mind not being wanted by WomenForms, but not being needed was a fate worse than death.

"You called for me, My Queen?" he asked, smiling broadly.

She returned his smile. It made him happy when she smiled at him. He'd known her since she was an InfantForm and had watched her grow from innocent and precocious into calculating and cold warrior. Over time, he'd seen more than a few false smiles plastered on her beautiful face.

Unlike Queen Vivant, she used her smiles as weapons. They meant life or death to the one receiving them—except him. She had always treated him with respect. Perhaps she remembered the small gardens he'd grown for her as a ChildForm.

Or when he'd brought succulent little treats pilfered from Princess Vivant's LifeCelebrations. Not everyone had agreed with King Dubian forbidding Princess Revari from attending.

He'd never married to sire children of his own. Like many unseen, unknown staff who worked in the grand halls of Platirius, he hadn't agreed with the abhorrent way King Dubian had treated his youngest daughter. Unlike his nemesis, he had adored little Princess Revari. Being mindful such thoughts were absurd and dangerous, he secretly wished he had fathered her.

On Platirius, commoners never married royalty. It was unheard of. As beautiful and kind as Queen Dellah was, he kept his thoughts to himself whenever she was around.

Since she loved the magnificent gardens he created, he had been one of the Coldarians she'd brought with her when she married King Dubian. Her death had been heart-wrenching, but it hadn't been the tiny princess's fault. No InfantForm should ever be blamed for the death of their MotherForm.

Did it bother him that Queen Revari had orchestrated the deaths of Queen Vivant's ChildForms? No. Neither she or King Dubian had assisted her when she needed protection. They chose to abandon her. Thus, she'd been exposed to excruciating pain she hadn't deserved.

Secrets. Long-dead secrets echoed through the ancient halls of Old Platirius. He suspected this was why it split when she succeeded in killing King Dubian. Too much had been done for Queen Revari to ever reign peacefully with her sister.

As respected as she was on both sides of Platirius, he didn't think much of Queen Vivant. In his eyes, she was spoiled, pampered, and had taken advantage of her position as the favorite ChildForm.

What King Dubian denied to his youngest daughter, he lavished on his firstborn. There were grand LifeCelebrations and shiny new crafts. He'd even given her his number one MaleForm in the Platirian army, General Kron.

Over time, Gallium's contempt for King Dubian slowly extended to his first daughter. He never saw her attempt to dissuade King Dubian from mistreating her sister. She hadn't pleaded with him to be kind to the younger princess. Not once.

Ultimately, she had turned a blind eye when Queen Revari had needed her the most. She had allowed her to suffer needlessly and even had the gall to blame Queen Revari for changing into who she was. It was rumored she blamed her for the death of their mother. Gallium didn't know, nor did he care.

The suffering heaped upon Queen Vivant was a cold dish she had prepared for consumption many years ago. Although he couldn't address her as an equal, he was proud of all Queen Revari had accomplished. He wanted her plan to succeed and would do anything to help her make it happen.

Queen Revari knew Gallium was a lifelong ally to her. While she couldn't say it, she loved him as the FatherForm she'd never had. He'd been there to wipe the many tears she'd shed in the past. Without him, she doubted she'd know how to smile genuinely as she was smiling at him now.

He had shown unquestionable allegiance to her. Now, she was so close to wiping Queen Vivant off the face of Platirius. She could almost taste the sweetness of victory. But not yet.

"Let's take a walk in the gardens," she suggested.

He bowed gracefully. "After you, your Highness."

As they walked side by side, the formidable queen and her loyal subject, the Revaltians saluted her as she passed. "Gallium, how long will it be before we can administer the Callidut to the Humans?"

"Well, there are over eight billion lifeforms on Earth. The easiest way to administer it is as you've planned—as a drug. Once you gain their trust by setting up the new company and getting investors on board, nothing will stop you from stocking it in medical centers and laboratories all over Earth. What's even better? The Humans will rob Peter to pay Paul to buy it."

She raised an amused eyebrow at his gift of learning the Human language. As a young MaleForm, he'd been sent on special missions to Earth. He'd learned every language they spoke—English, Spanish, French, Dutch, Korean—all of them. He passed his knowledge to a young Princess Revari whenever he returned from his missions.

King Dubian had never wanted her to advance. Shedding blood for Platirius was fine. Educating her—shaping her to think for herself—was not. However, he'd been too cowardly to confront Gallium for lavishing his attention on her.

Once she became queen, she had him teach the Revaltians. From slang to proper speech, they could go nowhere on Earth and be ignorant of its languages.

He kneeled down to pull a cluster of weeds from a row of dahlias. "They'll pay you for the very thing that will destroy them all in the end. The effects of Callidut are flawless—and—unstoppable. Even Queen Vivant won't be able to reverse its effects. That is, if she finds a way to escape from her mental hell."

"May I have that large dahlia?" asked Queen Revari. After placing it in her hair, they moved further into the gardens. "We've been giving her the Callidut for sixty days. One of the medical staff we planted in Platineous told me she was nauseous just before the LifeCelebration."

"Yes. Nausea is the first sign Callidut has taken over the bloodstream."

Working closely with Simonius, he ensured all doses created specifically for Queen Vivant were measured accurately.

"Visual and auditory hallucinations are the second phase caused by Callidut."

She unconsciously leaned into him, listening carefully.

"The third phase follows closely behind. That's when the cravings begin. The timing of the deaths was perfect. Soon, she'll begin seeing visions of her daughters while craving more Callidut. Now, she'll think she's just ravenous, but since we fashioned some of the Callidut into seasoning, food won't taste the same to her without it."

"What if someone else consumes the seasoning? What effect will it have on them?"

He shook his head. "None. Our technology can create substances specifically for a single body. Humans use biometrics like fingerprints, keystrokes, and facial recognition to commit frivolous acts such as stealing identities. As you know, My Queen, our technology is far more sophisticated. We use biometrics—veins, irises, and even blood types to create substances with uniquely specific effects only to the individual they were made for."

They rounded a life-sized statue of her. She had it built shortly after becoming queen.

"The Callidut sample we designed for Queen Vivant won't affect anyone other than her. Once introduced to her system, it learned everything in her body—blood vessels, cellular structure, and even the number of times synapses fire within her brain. The Callidut acts in the same manner a scanner recognizes a fingerprint. It only recognizes her DNA."

He looked up at the statue, pleased the queen's likeness was crafted perfectly.

"This is also how we manipulated the systems to allow the Human access to Platineous's halls. Our systems scan blood patterns unique to Platirians. The systems thought it was Queen Vivant entering the gardening and dining chambers, not a Human, so it let him pass. With Cia using her magic to provide a smokescreen over the cameras, the plan was perfectly executed. No matter how much the Vivacians try to uncover what happened, they won't succeed. Since it doesn't grow on Platineous, they know nothing of Callidut or its effects."

He answered her next question before she asked. "Simonius is no fool. He won't breathe a word to the Vivacians. Every MaleForm who survived the Mass Deaths understands it is you who allowed us to live. He would've followed King Dubian into the sun if Queen Vivant had her way. Simonius has not forgotten this. His allegiance is to you."

"It'd better be," she said. "You and Dr. Barrios are here on Rubarius, but Simonius is stationed on Platineous to keep an eye on Queen Vivant and her Vivacians."

She loved the breathtaking view of the royal gardens. Watching things grow had brought her tremendous peace during her ChildForm years. At times, the beauty and tranquility of the gardens had stopped her from losing her sanity.

She breathed in the magnificent perfume of the enormous, elaborate flowers, energized by their sweetness. "Does that silly little Vivacian still have a crush on him?"

He chuckled. "Yes, she does, My Queen. Along with a few others."

"And Simonius continues to rebuff her advances?"

"Yes, he's annoyed with her. He's aware she's not worth his life."

"Such weak WomenForms. Speaking of weak—General Lyric was raked over the coals for her incompetence in the justice chamber." She laughed heartily. "I thoroughly enjoyed that!"

He laughed with her. "You attended? Was Queen Vivant there?"

"Yes, I did, and no, she wasn't. She was undoubtedly laid up in her expensive bed chamber, endlessly wailing."

"It serves General Lyric right," he said. "She's always poking her nose where it doesn't belong. Just like her mother.

She looked at him curiously but when he didn't elaborate, she didn't press the issue. Some secrets were meant to stay buried."

"She has an air about her I just don't like. She's always believed she was better than General Legend. I'm glad she was finally put in her place."

"From your lips to The One's ears," muttered Queen Revari. She turned to him with a knowing glance. "Now we wait for the effects of the Callidut to begin working on her. Once she's declared incompetent, I will be appointed as the interim ruler of Platineous."

They reached the entrance of her palace. He bowed and opened the door for her. "And General Lyric isn't a royal. She won't be able to touch you."

"Mmm. I'm confident Queen Vivant isn't going to get better anytime soon. You and Dr. Barrios have your orders to keep her mind scrambled like eggs. That will leave me in charge long enough to prepare Earth for absorption. Then, Gallium? Platirius will be mine!" Her vibrant laugh rang out through the halls. "It's a perfect plan!" she exclaimed happily.

"I knew you could do it, Queen Revari. I've always had faith in you. You are the rightful heir to the throne of Platirius. It should solely belong to you."

"And it will," she said. "It's just a matter of time now."

The stars were illuminating the sky when Queen Vivant awakened in a cold sweat. She thought she heard one of her daughters calling to her. But how could that be? Her babies were gone. Wait. There it was again!

"Motheeeerrrrrr! Help meeeeeeeeeee!" *It was Princess Tarah! She was calling to her!* She sprang to her feet and ran to the window. *There! There she was! Her daughter!* Princess Tarah was looking up at her in panic.

"Help me, Mother!" she cried.

"I'm coming!" she shouted "I'm coming, Baby!" She'd kill whoever dared to hurt her precious daughter! Grabbing her BrainStaff, she ran out into the darkness of Space.

"General Lyric! Queen Vivant is running towards the Outer Realm!"

She put down the sandwich she was going to eat. "What?! What on Platirius for?!"

"I don't know. She's running towards something and calling out, but there's nothing there!"

It's happening again, she thought. *Once again, we're being plagued by something we cannot see.* "Vivacians!" she shouted. "Let's go! We're not about to let our queen down again!"

A unified roar vibrated through the surveillance chamber. "This time," said General Lyric, "we're ready!"

Nothing could prepare them for what they saw. Queen Vivant was ranting and raving about an unseen enemy taking Princess Tarah. General Lyric and the Vivacians had searched high and low on the lands of Platineous and found nothing.

She looked closely at Queen Vivant. Her eyes were wide and she was perspiring heavily. Something was wrong. Very wrong.

She looked...deranged. "My Queen, there's nothing here. We've searched everywhere and haven't found any enemies or Princess Tarah."

General Lyric knew they wouldn't find the princess. Only hours ago, they had seen her shipped away along with her sisters. Was Queen Vivant losing her mind? No! It wasn't possible.

She was the strongest Platirian she knew. She had always kept a cool head, especially in battle. It was just the shock of losing her daughters. She needed rest and she would be fine.

"Come, Queen Vivant, allow me to take you back to your bed chamber," said General Lyric, gently taking her elbow. But she viciously snatched it away from her.

"No!" she shouted. "My baby is out here wandering in the darkness! I have to bring her and her sisters home!"

"But Queen Vivant," said Captain Kourtney. "Princess Tarah is—" Her voice trailed off. Although everyone knew it was true, she couldn't bear to say it.

"Queen Vivant," said Sergeant Alicia. "We have no idea what you're feeling, but we're all here for you. Please let us help you."

Queen Vivant looked at her through eyes that made the Vivacians stand still. They had never realized how much she resembled Queen Revari in this crazed state.

A strange chill swept through them. Watching their revered queen teeter on the scales of madness made them shudder.

As the hairs stood up on her arms, General Lyric resisted the urge to shrink away from her. Once again, she gently grabbed her arm. "Queen Vivant, let's go back to the palace now. We'll get you some tea, and you can rest."

She swung her cold, brilliant, Queen Revari-like gaze to General Lyric. "I have to find my daughter. I'm not leaving until I do. And if you don't help me, Lyric, I will slit your throat."

The Vivacians gasped. She had never spoken to any of them that way before.

She held General Lyric's gaze. "Did you not hear me?!" she shouted. "Spread out and find my daughters. Now!"

General Lyric backed away from her. For hours, they'd searched the Outer Realm with her. Now they were ordered to find—what? What did Queen Vivant see they could not? She didn't know. What she did know was she was loyal to the throne of Platineous and its queen.

"Vivacians!" she ordered. "Let's spread out!"

After searching for five more hours, the Vivacians were just as exhausted as Queen Vivant. Her voice had become hoarse from yelling for Princess Tarah. Her movements became so sluggish that she could barely raise her BrainStaff.

"Taraaaaaaaaaaaah," she called again.

"Sergeant Thea," whispered General Lyric. "You have to run and get Dr. Barrios. We can't stay out here all night. We've searched for hours and have found nothing! Something is wrong with Queen Vivant. I don't know what it is, but we must help her. And be discreet. This is no time to create a panic. The last thing we need is to put Queen Revari in a position to rule over us all, even temporarily."

"Yes, General!" said Sergeant Thea.

Before she could move, Queen Vivant cried, "I'm hungry! I'm so very hungry!"

"Yes, Queen Vivant!" said General Lyric, running towards her. "Let's get some food for you, alright?"

"Yes, thank you, General Lyric. That would be wonderful!"

For the second time that night, the Vivacians were shocked. Queen Vivant had a strange, vacant look in her eyes. She acted as if she'd forgotten why she was in the Outer Realm.

General Lyric decided she didn't have time to figure it out. They had to get her back to Platineous. "Come, Queen Vivant, we'll call for a midnight supper."

The Vivacians wondered when the shock was going to wear off. It certainly wasn't anytime soon. They stared in horror as Queen Vivant devoured a feast set for three MaleForms.

In less than an hour, she'd eaten two porterhouse steaks, a small roasting chicken, half of a ham, four twice-baked potatoes, a serving bowl of mixed greens with baby heirloom tomatoes, cucumbers, mushrooms, carrots, and chives, and an entire apple pie. She drank a whole pitcher of PotterBerry juice to wash down the enormous meal.

It wasn't just the volume of food that amazed the warriors. It was how she ate. Queen Vivant usually had impeccable table manners, yet she had refused to use cutlery, opting to eat with her hands. Repeatedly, she stuffed food in her mouth like a ravenous lioness. The Vivacians had never seen her behave in such a manner.

Spent, she finally scooted away from the dining table. Wiping her potato-covered fingers across her mouth, she said, "I'm tired. General Lyric, I am so very tired."

General Lyric assisted her to her bed chamber. Instantly, she climbed atop her elaborate bed and slept. This was also out of character for her. She was adamant about bathing before bedtime and was a stickler for cleanliness.

She didn't tolerate spots or spills throughout the halls of her palace. Now, she couldn't have cared less about the grease, butter, and stickiness from her late-night meal covering her pristine bed covers. The Vivacians looked sadly at her before looking helplessly at General Lyric.

"Do you still want me to get Dr. Barrios?" asked Sergeant Thea.

She swallowed tightly. She didn't trust Dr. Barrios. She'd only ordered it in a moment of weakness out of not knowing what to do to assist the WomanForm she'd sworn allegiance to in her eighteenth summer.

"No. There's no need to call him now. She just needed to eat. Now, we'll let her rest. Our queen will be in much better shape tomorrow," she assured the Vivacians.

Queen Vivant will be better tomorrow, thought General Lyric. She had to be.

Chapter 6

S he was wrong. By dawn, Queen Vivant had awakened starving and even more ludicrous than she had been the previous night. A large, sumptuous meal of bacon, fried potatoes with onions, and scrambled eggs was set before her.

At the queen's request, stacks of steaming, fluffy pancakes dripping with butter and maple syrup, accompanied by slabs of ham covered in honey were also added to her dining table. Queen Vivant washed it all down with large pitchers of fresh milk and apple juice.

The dining staff marveled at the queen's voracious appetite. They'd never seen her eat so much.

This had to be grief, thought Sgt. Thea.

After she consumed her small feast, she swiped the plate of a surprised Vivacian soldier and ate every last bit of the food.

Dr. Barrios smoothly entered the dining chamber and watched as she devoured the food. As he observed her behavior, General Lyric never took her eyes off him. He knew something. She could tell by the smugness in his eyes.

Suddenly, he felt he was being watched. He swung his eyes over to General Lyric, hastily pasting on a false look of concern.

The queen's general was too observant for her own good. No WomanForm, especially her, would outwit him.

"How long has she been acting this way?" he asked.

"Since last night. She's been ravenous and searching for—" Her gaze returned to Queen Vivant. Quickly, she lowered her tone. "She's convinced Princess Tarah is still alive. She had us looking for her for half the night before she became exhausted. She finally allowed us to bring her inside to sleep."

Queen Vivant's crisp tone cut their conversation short. "Why are you whispering to a MaleForm about my business?"

General Lyric gasped. "My Queen, I was just filling him in about—"

Giving her a frosty gaze, she cut her off. "Who are you to report to a common MaleForm about me? Do you realize that were it not for me, you wouldn't be the leader of my army?"

She was taken aback by her queen's tone and the cold, steady gaze of her silver eyes. She sounded exactly like Queen Revari!

"Yes, My Queen, I know, and I'm truly grateful for your generosity," she said.

"Lyric, did I make a mistake in choosing you to lead my army? If I had selected better, would my beloved daughters still be alive?"

Tears stung in her eyes. She could take accusations from the council and Queen Revari. Yet, she could not abide Queen Vivant twisting the knife already stuck in her heart.

As Queen Vivant fell silent, Dr. Barrios stared at her in horror. A change in appetite and hallucinations were expected, yes. But a change in her personality? Her mannerisms were eerily similar to her sister's. He'd never imagined the Callidut would clone her into another Queen Revari. He didn't believe Platineous and Rubarius could survive two WomenForms with her personality.

Suddenly, her cheeks puffed up. Dr. Barrios watched as she threw back her head, cackling maniacally.

She's truly lost her mind!

Devoid of the warmth it once possessed, her soft chuckle rang hollow among the young WomenForms under her leadership. "At ease, General Lyric! I'm jesting with you! My daughters are alive, you silly fool! And you and my Vivacians are going to find them. Today." Her brilliant smile faded. "Or I'll ship the lot of you off into the sun."

The stillness in the room matched her tone. Chilly. Dark. Foreboding. Oblivious to the sheer terror she had just struck in the hearts of her soldiers, she continued.

"My babies. They're playing a horrific joke on their MotherForm. After all I've done for them. They shall be beaten before all of Platirius for their treachery."

General Lyric stifled a gasp. Now she sounded like King Dubian. He'd taken great pleasure in stripping WomenForms and having them beaten for the slightest infractions. Even worse, he ordered it to be done in the middle of Platirius for all to see.

Queen Dellah's death had driven him insane. Now, something similar was happening to Queen Vivant. How deeply did madness run in the royal bloodline?

Silently, Dr. Barrios shared General Lyric's thoughts. He breathed a sigh of relief that the Callidut blocked Queen Vivant from reading minds.

"Your Highness, I was wondering if you'd come to the medical chamber and allow me to look at you."

At this, she raised an eyebrow. "For what reason? I'm not unwell, Dr. Barrios. Perhaps you are searching for an excuse to see me unclothed? Do you believe I'm stupid enough to allow that?"

He knew better than to challenge her. In this state, she wasn't as amicable and carefree as she once was. "You are alive by Queen Revari's order, not mine. I told her you should've died along with the other MaleForms, but she wouldn't hear of it. We had no WomenForm physicians then, so I agreed to her order for you to remain on Platirius."

When she sat and crossed her legs, a flash of Queen Dellah entered his mind. "But that order has outlived its time, hasn't it? We have more than enough skilled WomenForm physicians to replace you. Not that it was hard to do. Your incompetence couldn't even keep my father alive," she said bitterly.

"I don't think that'll be necessary, sister," a familiar voice chimed in.

Every head turned towards Queen Revari, resplendent in a dazzling new outfit.

"You're all dressed up," noted Queen Vivant. "Have you finally decided to attend my daughters' LifeCelebration once we find them?"

She didn't bat an eyelash. "Of course. We've been getting along so well I decided to take your olive branch. But first, we must ensure you're well enough to go."

"I feel fine. I'll feel even better once my daughters are found." She looked at General Lyric. "See to it."

She led the Vivacians out of the dining chamber at her queen's command. She didn't want to go, but she was powerless against Queen Revari. She had no choice except to leave her in her sister's cold, unfeeling hands.

Queen Revari glanced at Dr. Barrios before focusing on Queen Vivant once more. "You're aware we must have royal examinations once a year. It's rude to use your daughters' unruliness as an excuse to skip it."

"They've snuck off in their crafts before, but they've never been gone this long."

Queen Revari wrinkled her nose. So, it was true. She truly was losing her mind. After Dr. Barrios had sent word to her, she hastened to see her sister's descent into madness for herself. To her knowledge, the princesses had never disobeyed their mother's orders. Not once. The little cowards.

Nor had she spoken ill of her daughters. It wasn't in her nature. It seemed the Callidut was fulfilling its purpose. Her bizarre ramblings contradicted her usual poised and graceful articulation. Queen Revari couldn't be happier.

She kept talking until she convinced her to visit the medical chamber. Away from the watchful eyes of General Lyric and the

Vivacians, she had her sedated and examined by Dr. Barrios. The results of her lab work were conclusive and promising.

She ordered the royal attendants to bathe her and dress her in a fresh day gown. They stripped the bedding from the night before and laid her atop fresh sheets and comforters. She'd be out for hours. When she awakened, she would barely remember her name. Queen Revari had finally succeeded in her plans to ensure she wouldn't get in the way of her mission.

Before dawn, Queen Revari awakened to a visibly shaken Chief Counselor Adoni on her TranScreen.

"I haven't had my breakfast, Adoni!" she snapped. "What could you possibly want at this hour?"

"It's Queen Vivant! She's attempted to open a portal to let the Kikhanians into Platineous!"

Her mouth dropped. Planet Kikhani was the home of their most formidable opponents. Major Kron had become a general when his predecessor was killed in battle by the Kikhanians. It was the only time Platirius had come close to being defeated. Following his superior military tactics, Platirius was victorious against Kikhani.

He designed the protective shield around Platirius—a door closed only to the Kikhanians. The shield was never to be opened. Now, her narcotized, hallucinating sister nearly opened the gateway for them to go to war again.

She wanted to wrap her hands around Queen Vivant's neck and squeeze until her eyes bulged out of their sockets. The last thing she needed was to be forced to deal with the demented Kikhanians. They truly had no soul!

She swore under her breath. "Why did she try to open it?"

"She believes her daughters are being held captive by the Kikhanians," said Chief Counselor Adoni. "She has mobilized the Vivacians to go and retrieve them! Queen Revari, she's completely ludicrous!"

"Where is she now?"

"The Vivacians have her locked away in her bed chamber. They quickly removed her from the surveillance chamber before she opened the portal."

She let out a long sigh. "Thank goodness! How did General Lyric allow this to happen?! I've always known she was incompetent, but this? We cannot afford to go to war with the Kikhanians!"

She threw back her bed covers and hastily dressed in a silk robe. "To defeat them, I'd need both armies. She is still in charge of Platineous!"

Her stomach growled. Couldn't Queen Vivant have waited until she'd eaten before she tried to bring them to ruin?

"I'm aware, and as of now, the council has decided to temporarily remove Queen Vivant and appoint you to rule

Platineous until she becomes well again. General Lyric is still the leader of the Vivacian army."

"General Lyric! If I didn't know better, I'd think she planned for this. She's a commoner who worked her way up the ranks. She knows she'll never rule Platirius, so this is the next best scenario."

"That may be, but she's now under your authority. No commoner may rule over a royal. She understands this is a temporary assignment."

Rubbing her temples, she cursed her sister. She almost wrecked everything! She hadn't expected the Callidut would make her crazy enough to roll out a red carpet across Space for the most lethal of their enemies.

"General Legend!" she called.

Immediately, General Legend appeared. "Yes, Queen Revari."

"Order my staff to run my bath and prepare my breakfast. If I'm going to witness my sister looking like a deranged fool in front of Platineous, I will look and feel my best doing it."

"Yes, My Queen. Right away."

After a refreshing bath, she was seated at her grand dining table munching on fat slabs of pork belly, accompanied by bowls of jasmine rice and rich broth. She wasn't a bit sorry for planning Queen Vivant's downfall.

The princesses of Platirius had unwrapped a present that traveled through time to reach them—karma. She meant what she said to General Lyric. She wasn't responsible for their deaths—their mother was. In another time, Queen Vivant had set everything in motion.

She'd still have her daughters if she had kept her nose out of her business when they were younger. And—Queen Revari would still have—him. *No*, she thought. *Not now.* She could not—would not think of him now. He'd been gone for too long.

As hard as she tried not to become overwhelmed by her past, at times, memories of him rolled across her mind like waves, threatening to drown her in sorrow. She willed her mind to think more positively. At the moment, she was having too much fun to mourn.

Finally, Queen Vivant was getting precisely what she deserved. Queen Revari only wished he were around to see it. She longed to see his face. Touch him. Hear his laugh again. Yet, it wasn't to be. Her family had taken away everyone she'd ever loved. She'd paid her father back in spades. Now it was her sister's turn.

M oments later, she graced the halls of Platineous. Shocked, sad faces glanced her way as she made her grand entrance and locked eyes with Queen Vivant, who stared back at her. For a moment, time stood still as everyone wondered what Queen Vivant would do next.

"Mother!" cried Queen Vivant. "You're here! You finally made it to my LifeCelebration!"

Queen Revari stopped in midstride. Not even she had been prepared for this change in her. She was the spitting image of Queen Dellah. King Dubian had never allowed her to see a photo of her, but Queen Vivant clearly remembered how she looked.

In the confines of her mind, overloaded by the effects of Callidut, she truly believed her mother was standing before her. Queen Revari gaped at her for a few moments. Realizing the unplanned bewilderment caused by the eerie declaration worked in her favor, she turned her attention to General Lyric, meeting her with a spiteful gaze.

"You allowed this to happen! I've never seen a general as stupid and incompetent as you! The queen of Platineous running around like a bumbling fool, nearly exposing us to our enemies! It's inexcusable!"

"What's Platineous, Mother?" asked Queen Vivant innocently. "And who is this queen?"

"Fetch a day gown for her, you idiot!" Queen Revari called to Tiko, a Vivacian soldier.

She snatched the expensive gown from her hands. "Put this on, Vivant."

"Yes, Mother!" she said happily as Queen Revari dressed her.

The Vivacians were all scared and saddened by what was happening to their leader. Grief had caused her to lose her mind. Grief, they knew, was more terrible of a weapon than any sword or BrainStaff.

The council of justice appeared on a large TranScreen. "Queen Revari," said Chief Counselor Adoni. "The council believes it will be quite a long time before Queen Vivant is ready to return to her duties."

She stared coldly at the Chief Counselor. "That much is clear, Adoni. The thought of the Kikhanians once again setting foot on Platirius makes me physically ill. This must never happen again."

"I agree. We didn't realize it would get this bad," said the Chief Counselor.

She sighed. "No one could have predicted this," she said. "It's up to me to keep all of Platirius safe." She gave a withering glance to General Lyric. *General Legend and my Revaltians will undoubtedly have their hands full.*

"You," she said pointing at General Lyric. "Keep Queen Vivant in her bed chamber," she ordered. "Make sure she is under tight security. Have her meals brought to her. She must not be permitted to roam about without my permission."

After observing her more closely, she held back a squeal of laughter. Her face and arms were covered in scratches, and one eye was swelling into a purple bulb.

That's what she got for trying to remove Queen Vivant from the surveillance chamber and escort her to her bed chamber where she'd be safe. Now, safe was the last thing the Vivacians would feel again. Once she claimed Earth, they'd be the first to enter the sun.

"Any requests to me go through General Legend. You are not permitted to contact me for any reason. She'll be briefed about my sister's health and safety every hour. As of now, you and all of the Vivacians answer to me. Is anything I've just ordered unclear in your mind, General Lyric?"

"No, Queen Revari. Your orders are crystal clear."

"Then get to it. Oh, and one more thing? One more slip-up and I'll demote you to Private. You got that?"

With a heavy heart, she saluted her. "Yes, Queen Revari! I am ready to serve at your command!"

She smiled venomously. "That's a good dog, General Lyric. You may go now. I want to sit with my sister for a moment."

"Mother, why must I stay in bed?" asked Queen Vivant.

Queen Revari looked at her, energized by the rapid decline of her mental health. She thought she was in her teens. At least for today, she'd forgotten about her daughters. Now that she had free reign over Platineous, she made a mental note to remind Gallium to process more of the Callidut root.

"Because you're gravely ill," she said smoothly. "Being out in the winds without proper clothing has made you unwell. You don't want to pass an illness on to your friends, do you?"

She frowned and sniffed. "I guess not," she said.

"That's right. Now, I want you to be good and listen to Mother, understand?" She watched her nod. "Excellent. Now lie down and take a nap. I'll have your luncheon brought up in a few hours."

Truthfully, she had no idea how Queen Dellah would've handled her daughter had she fallen ill. Only Gallium had been brave enough to share bits of information about her mother with her. She learned she'd been a kind, gentle queen who wanted the best for Platirius and its people.

Queen Revari also wanted the best. For herself. Since she'd grown up alone, without close friends and family to interact with, she'd grown into a self-absorbed young WomanForm.

That was until she met *him*. He was the first Human she'd ever seen and spoken to. He, who grew up in a loving family with lots of friends, showed her a wonderous new existence she'd never imagined.

U nable to bear any more of King Dubian's intolerance, she was sixteen summers when she ran away from Platirius. Always the independent rebel, she taught herself to drive a craft at fifteen. Although she'd explored other planets, she had never been to Earth.

She crashed the craft in a place called Miami, Florida. Quickly, she punched in the code that would render it invisible to the Human eye and got out.

No one had heard him calling for help except her. The crash's impact had knocked him into a deep hole he couldn't get out of. She remembered the first time she had seen him.

He was tall and olive-skinned. His curly black hair was thick and wavy. He had deep impressions on both sides of his cheeks, which he later informed her were *dimples*. His name was Oliver Ascencio—an odd name—she thought.

She'd heard stories about Humans from the staff who had snuck into her nursery chamber to watch them on the TranScreen. It was the only place King Dubian didn't have under surveillance. He had loathed the sight of his youngest daughter.

According to the staff, the Humans were evil Beings. Liars. Rapists. Murderers. They hated everyone and everything, including themselves. They called Platirians and every Being outside of Earth a nasty name—*Aliens*—as if they were dirty and inferior.

The gall! As the least intelligent Beings in the galaxy, it was they who were unclean and inferior! Humans had no respect for the sanctity of life. Not on their planet or anywhere in the galaxy. They were violent, intolerant, and sneaky.

And so, no population outside Earth's realm had ever attempted to make peace with them. It would be a waste of time. If they could not tolerate each other's perceived differences, why would they extend kindness and mercy to those who did not belong to Earth?

Galactic Beings were content with watching them make fools of themselves on their TranScreens. Little did the Humans know that while they watched each other for entertainment, they were the primary source of entertainment around the galaxy.

Princess Revari kept this in mind as she slowly moved closer to the hole where the Human was trapped. She reached the edge and peered down into it. She gasped when she saw him. Long eyelashes surrounded his piercing green eyes. They widened when she appeared.

"Hey!" he called. "Can you get me out of here?"

Raising an impertinent brow, she asked, "Why should I?"

Incredulously, he gaped in the direction of the voice. "Because I was walking and minding my own business when a loud explosion blew me into this hole! It's not my fault I'm down here!"

"Are you saying it's mine?" she asked.

"Did you make the explosion?"

She thought about that for a moment. "Well—I suppose."

"Okay. Then it's your fault!" he cried.

"That doesn't mean I have to get you out."

He shook his head in disbelief. "You have to get me out. I'll die if I stay down here."

"Isn't that what you're supposed to do? Die before all other LifeForms? What would it matter if you died sooner than you expected?"

Ay dios! LifeForms? What in the world was she talking about?

"Are you psychotic or something?"

She paused to pick a lovely flower. Sniffing it, she sneezed. It smelled nothing like the flowers on Platirius. "What does psychotic mean?"

Was she serious? "Are you a psycho?!" he exclaimed. "A nut! Crazy!"

"Are you insulting me?" she asked suspiciously.

"Oh God," he groaned. "Please tell me this is a bad dream."

"I'm no dream. I am very real, Human."

"Human? Did you just call me a Human? I don't know how to break this to you, but you're a Human too! And a crazy one at that!"

Incensed, she glared at him. "I'm no Human! If you insult me again, I'll break your neck!"

He couldn't believe his ears. "Oh man—you are crazy, aren't you? Did you break out of the mental hospital or something?"

"That's it!" she shouted before jumping into the hole. Running toward him at full force, she shoved him hard in the chest. As expected, he dropped like a stone.

Stunned, he tried to get back on his feet. Not only was the girl unhinged, she was violent. He tried to diffuse the situation before things got out of hand. "Hey! Come on! I don't fight girls! Calm down, okay?"

"Don't tell me to calm down!"

He groaned, rubbing his chest. She was pretty strong for a girl. His father had warned him never to tell a girl to calm down. It only made them worse. This girl—at least she sounded like a girl—was unbalanced.

He had to think fast, or she'd leave him there. No one knew where he was, and it might take days to find him. He'd be dead by then. Changing tactics, he tried to appeal to her more subtly.

"Listen, we both can't get trapped down here, okay? I don't want to die and I'm sure you don't either."

Her tone was smug. "I can get out of here on my own. It is you who cannot."

She may be right about that, he thought, getting to his feet. Something hard struck him on his thigh.

She pointed to the large stick she threw at him and said, "Pick up your weapon and fight like a MaleForm."

"A MaleForm? What's that?"

"MaleForms live on my planet. And you? You're a loathsome Human. Now fight me!"

Shaking his head, he said, "I'm not going to fight you. I don't fight girls." He paused. "You *are* a girl, aren't you?"

"I'm a WomanForm," she said proudly. "Today is the day of my sixteenth summer!"

Ohhh man. "Okay...well...happy birthday! I'm Oliver and I just turned seventeen last month." His anxiety increased at her silence. "It's—nice to meet you," he stammered. "I'm sorry if I hurt your feelings. I'm not a rude person, honestly. I'm pretty cool and easy to get along with." He realized he was talking a mile a minute while she remained silent. "What's your name?"

"I am Princess Revari."

Stay calm. Just keep her talking so she'll get you out of this hole.

"I already told you I'm not going to help you."

Did she just read my mind?? No way! Calm down, Oliver! One of you has to be rational!

"Do you always talk to yourself in your mind?"

Now it was he who was silent—and scared.

"No need to stop now. I can hear every word you think."

This is NOT happening.

She was delighted by his discomfort. "Oh, but it is happening. Now, pick up your weapon. You shall be punished for insulting your better."

My better? "I can't see it," he said flatly.

"Why not? It's right at your feet and..." she paused, looking up at the sky, "...darkness hasn't descended upon us yet."

He decided not to focus on the strange way she spoke. Something told him lying to her wouldn't help either.

"I can't see the stick or you. I'm blind."

Sensing he wasn't lying, she peered at him in the dark. "What is blind?"

For once, he was thankful he was a patient person. "My eyes don't work."

For the first time, she was curious about this strange Human. "Why not?"

Quickly, he tried to clear his mind. If she could read his mind, he didn't want to make her angrier than she already was.

"I don't know," he admitted. "I've been this way since I was born."

"And you're still alive? Your father didn't kill you for being weak?"

He forgot about not angering her. "I'm not weak!" he shouted. "And my dad would never hurt me for being blind!"

"You just said you cannot see. You don't think that is a weakness? How do you care for yourself?"

"I take care of myself just fine! I was walking—by myself—when you made that loud blast. I lost my cane and ended up here. Ah! My cane!"

Quickly, he scrambled to his knees, searching wildly in the dirt for it. "You said it was by my feet. I can't find it."

Revari grabbed the stick and gave it to him. "Is that better?" she asked.

"Yes, thank you."

"Now we'll fight!"

"This isn't a weapon," he informed her. It's to help me get around. I use it to keep my balance and not run into things—or fall. Listen—Princess Reverie."

She frowned. "It's Princess Re-var-ee."

"Okay, fine—I'm sorry I mispronounced it, Princess Revari? And I'm sorry I insulted you. Please, I'm not a fighter. I'm really a nice guy. Can we start over?"

She looked around the hole. If he couldn't see, he wouldn't be able to get out and tell others about her. "Why would I want to do that? What's in it for me?"

Puzzled, he furrowed his brows, struggling to find a way to escape from her. "Well...what do you want?"

She nodded at the jewelry he wore around his wrist. "That bracelet will do."

"My dad gave this to me," he protested.

"I don't care who gave it to you. Give it to me. Right now."

Quickly, he took it off and handed it to her. "You sure are bossy, aren't you?"

"Of course. One day, I'll take over Platirius and become queen."

Oliver decided not to comment on that. "Aren't you going to say thank you?"

"To a Human? Don't make me vomit."

Oliver sighed. This girl was unlike anyone he'd ever met in his life. "Alright. I gave you my chain. Now, can you get me out here, please?"

Princess Revari decided she liked the bracelet. And she wanted to know more about the Human Oliver, so she said, "Okay, you're free now."

"But we haven't moved!"

"Yes, we have," she said, still admiring the bracelet. "Walk around with your stick and you'll know."

Sure enough, as Oliver tentatively explored his surroundings, he realized he was out of the hole. But how? He hadn't moved from the spot he'd been standing in.

Who is she?

"Now, Human Oliver," said Princess Revari. "You're going to tell me everything about you. And do it quickly."

As the evening drew to a close, she learned about ice cream, hip-hop, Latin music, Thanksgiving and Christmas, and so much more. She discovered what it meant to be blind. What he lacked in sight, he made up with a sparkling personality she genuinely found engaging.

He kept up a lively conversation and told jokes she didn't quite understand, but they made her laugh anyway. An unfamiliar feeling crept over her. She had no name for it but decided she enjoyed it. Very much.

Oliver enjoyed talking to her as well. After he finished telling another joke, he heard crickets chirping. It was getting late. His mother would start to worry if he wasn't home soon.

He didn't know why, but he didn't want to leave. She spoke strangely and her thoughts were equally as strange. Still, she was unique. Captivating. She smelled of sweet things, too—cinnamon, lemon, and sugar cookies.

"What perfume are you wearing?" he suddenly asked.

"What is perfume?"

"It's a scent you spray on your body. It makes you smell good."

"I don't need that. My scent belongs to me."

He didn't know if he believed her, but if she could read his mind, why would she lie about her scent?

"I don't lie. I have no reason to lie."

He decided then and there he'd try to believe everything she told him. Maybe she wasn't human. Maybe it was he who was crazy. He didn't know and was too tired to figure it out.

"I have to go home now, Princess Revari. It's getting late."

Princess Revari's interest piqued again. "Where is home?" she asked. She listened as he told her where he lived.

"Where's your home?" he asked.

"On Platirius. A planet very far from here. But I ran away."

He nodded and filed that bit of information away for later. "Would you like to come home with me? My sister is away at college. You could sleep in her room. It's just me and my parents now."

"Okay, let us go."

And so they went. She met his parents and ate the peculiar food they served. She particularly liked dishes they called *pernil* and *rice with black beans*. A vegetable salad with robust flavors and a thick, creamy concoction called *flan* completed the meal.

Human Oliver's parents had been very nice to her—even Human Oliver's father. Human Oliver's mother showed her a beautifully decorated room—though not as grand and luxurious as her room on Platirius—and said she could sleep there.

She thought the parents were quite odd. They kept smiling at her, each other, and Human Oliver. They seemed genuinely happy she was there. It was all so very unfamiliar to Princess Revari. Why were Human Oliver's parents happy to have a child who could not see?

Over time, she learned what *love* was and what it meant to be a part of a loving family. She grew to be happy with the Ascencios. That is, until King Dubian found her. And her sister was to blame.

Queen Revari sat next to Queen Vivant as she slept. She got up and turned off the light, pausing to look down at her.

She didn't have an ounce of regret over what was happening to her. Queen Vivant had earned everything she was getting—and more. How wonderful it would be to send her off into the blazing sun.

Perhaps stuffed tightly in a death craft with General Lyric. No—that wouldn't do. She wanted her to suffer for as long as she had breath. Sending her to live out the afterlife with The One would be too kind. She had no intention of granting peace to her. Ever.

General Legend met her at the entrance leading out of Platineous. "You've done well, Queen Revari," she said. "Of course, I knew you would. I've fought enough battles by your side to know you always get the job done."

She looked up at a window, peering as if she could see into Queen Vivant's bed chamber. "I knew the Callidut was powerful, but I never thought it would alter her mind this severely."

"Yes. It's been the blessing I've prayed for. And the Ashion, of course."

"Now we'll start distributing the Callidut on Earth?" asked General Legend.

"Of course," said Queen Revari, smiling to herself. "But we'll call it another name. I intend to absorb Earth into Platirius in less than two of Earth's years."

General Legend nodded before looking up to the night sky, filled with brilliant stars.

"What will we do if The One intervenes?" she asked.

"He won't," said Queen Revari confidently. "As you saw, He didn't bother to assist Queen Vivant, His so-called appointed Protector of Earth. He allowed her to open a gateway to the Kikhanians. Without us, the Vivacians would've easily been defeated."

General Legend's eyes were still on the bed chamber. "I've stationed some of our Revaltians in the surveillance chamber. They'll stop her if she tries to open the shield again."

Queen Revari nodded. "That's why you're the better general over Lyric. You think with your head instead of your heart. Rest assured if He didn't help a Platirian queen, He'll do what He's always done for the Humans, leave them to their own devices. It's what He does best, General Legend."

As they looked out into the darkness of Space, a star soared to epic heights before falling helplessly into the night.

Epilogue

J ulia Gonzales was tired. It had been a long day. She sat down to watch the news and eat.

"The FDA has just approved a new drug to help combat obesity. Allebri, short for Allebrizapine, is gaining momentum as stories pour in concerning rapid weight loss without complications."

Sounds like a scam, thought Julia.

"That's right, people are claiming there are almost no side effects to Allebrizapine. Patients have reported not only has it helped them to lose a significant amount of weight, but it gives them a noticeably youthful appearance."

Intrigued, Julia turned up the volume.

"What people love most about the drug is there are no dietary restrictions and no need for strenuous exercise. Patients say they eat whatever they want and still shed weight."

Wait. I wouldn't have to give up pizza and ice cream?

"According to scientific studies, Allebrizapine is safe to take for as long as needed. It's produced by the manufacturer Rubarion Industries."

Julia took a bite of brisket and turned up the volume.

"Rubarion Industries is a newcomer to the market for weight loss drugs. Still, it has a solid record of successfully providing the health industry with life-saving medical devices. The company's founder, Dr. Revari Ascencio, is a second-generation heiress."

"Wow, she's gorgeous," said Julia. "I wonder if she's been taking Allebri."

The anchorwoman's voice buzzed with excitement. "Rubarion Industries's total earnings for its second quarter have surpassed its competitors at a record of over twelve billion dollars. Allebrizapine started slow, yet steady. It is now the most popular drug in the world."

Julia quickly set aside the heaping plate of brisket, mac and cheese, sweet potatoes, green beans, and cornbread. When you looked up "foodie" in the dictionary, her face should have been front and center.

She had dieted since she was eight. At thirty-six, all she was left with were aching knees and a slow metabolism. Being born into a family of tall, svelte women certainly had not been easy for her.

Over the years, her mother's nagging about her weight became the norm. She never made her youngest daughter feel beautiful. Guys had passed her up for prom, college, and eventually all of her friends' weddings.

She'd never had a real boyfriend. For Julia, the road to marriage and motherhood seemed very dim. Over the years, she'd tried almost everything on the market to lose weight. Even when she was successful, she always gained it back—plus more.

After the horrible experience she'd had the last time, she swore she'd never use any more weight loss drugs. But after hearing about Allebri, she wavered toward trying again. Was it possible she wouldn't have to deal with any side effects? Allebrizapine—where had she heard that before? Judy! Last month, Judy had been raving about it at the company Christmas party.

At the time, Julia tuned out of the conversation. She hadn't been interested in hearing about Judy's latest dieting phase. Now she was curious. She'd just have to call her and get the tea.

"Hey Judy, it's Julia!"

"Oh, hi!" said Judy. "What's up, Julia?"

"Remember that weight loss drug you told us about? I just heard about it on the news and was wondering if you could fill me in?"

"Oh girl, let me tell you! You're going to love it! I've lost so much weight, Alex can't keep his hands off me!"

Julia laughed. "Ummm, that's too much information. I just need to know about Allebrizapine."

"Oh, Allebri is fabulous!" said Judy. "It's a game changer!"

After chatting with Judy for about a half hour, Julia decided to make an appointment with her doctor to discuss being prescribed Allebrizapine. She was over forty pounds overweight and had struggled to lose weight all of her life. She was confident she'd be a good candidate. And, she had to admit, Judy looked fabulous!

She couldn't explain why Judy looked younger. She simply did. Judy had no skin hanging off her arms and legs, nor did her face look weird. Just an enhanced beauty she hadn't had before taking the drug. Could Allebri be the answer to her prayers? She didn't know, but she intended to find out.

Platirius: The Rise of Reve Book II

"Dr. Ascensio," said Aimee. "I'm all out of the Allebri."

Revari knew precisely when she'd run out of product. Gallium made concise doses. No one ever received more than they should've.

"And? What does that have to do with me? We gave you the product to promote and you did. Your job with us is finished."

She started to move around Aimee when she seized her arm in a vise-like grip. She looked down at the offending hand.

"You want to remove your hand or should I break it?" asked Revari softly.

Surprised, she quickly dropped her hand from her arm. What happened to the kind woman who had hired her? She held it up as if her desperation would stop Revari from walking away.

"Dr. Ascencio, please? I feel terrible. My insurance doesn't cover Allebri. It's the only thing that makes me feel good. Please give me more."

Unmoved, she surveyed her. "Then you can buy it like anyone else. What happened to all the money we gave you?"

Tears welled in Aimee's eyes. "I spent it all to get more Allebri."

And she had. In fact, she'd lost everything she acquired working for Rubarion Industries. The fancy loft overlooking the water, the expensive clothes and jewelry, even the new car she bought. In the end, all were hocked to buy more Allebri.

"Well, that sounds like a you problem, kid. We just hired five more British influencers. I have no more use for you."

"I'm begging you. Please give me a chance."

"I already gave you one. How did you repay me? You ended up being a junkie. Look at yourself."

She held up a Platirian mirror to Aimee's face. Horrified by her reflection, she started wailing.

"If I had more Allebri, it would fix this!" she declared. "Please! I need more!"

Now I have you. "What will you give me if I give you more, Aimee?"

"Anything! Anything you want!"

Her desperation excited her. "Will your soul do?"

Startled, Aimee stood still. "What?"

"You heard me. Are you willing to give me your soul for more Allebri?"

She didn't hesitate. "Yes! Take it! It's yours! Just give me more please."

That's music to my ears.

Aimee saw her eyes change from a dazzling gray to a strange bright red. As she gazed into Revari's eyes, transfixed by the peculiar, crimson glow, she heard a range of voices in her head, chanting in a language she could not understand.

She felt worse than she did when she woke up. Suddenly, the voices stopped and her mind cleared. The terrible feeling she'd had for weeks was finally gone.

She handed her a box of Allebri. "This will be enough to last for a while. Call me when you feel better, and we'll get you back on board with making more content for us. We appreciate all your hard work, Aimee."

Sighing with relief, she hugged the box tightly to her chest. "Thank you so much, Dr. Ascencio!"

Revari smiled like a crooked politician. "It's my pleasure, Aimee. You had this coming."

Her joyful smile widened as she stepped off the curb and walked in front of an oncoming bus. She was killed instantly.

D.L.'s Note

D ear Reader,

Did you enjoy your first journey to Platirius? I certainly hope
so! I genuinely enjoyed developing the characters you've read
about. Family dynamics are sometimes tricky. The Platirius
series was inspired by a need to cope with the personal struggles
that many of us face. I was inspired to create the Platirius series
to give hope to anyone who has ever felt as if they didn't belong.

While Platirius is a fictional world, the dynamics within the
story may connect with many readers. Not all families sit around
the fireplace during the holidays or gather annually for family
reunions. Queen Revari's story isn't unique. If you've ever
connected with terms such as 'outcast' or 'black sheep of the
family,' then Platirius is the series for you.

Platirius: The Rise of Reve is up next! I invite you to continue
reading the Platirius trilogy. You may discover you have an

intimate connection with one or more of the characters I've written. I also encourage you to embrace your unique identity and dare to create spaces when others claim there's not enough room for your individuality.

xoxo D.L.

Author Bio

D.L. Hannah was born in Youngstown, Ohio. She is a writer, entrepreneur, and host of the Amerisogyny podcast. She is a Psi Chi and Alpha Kappa Delta member and earned a Bachelor of Arts degree in Clinical Community Psychology from Walsh University. For over twenty years, she has been a strong advocate for children diagnosed with Autism. She now lives in North Carolina with her family.

Also by D.L. Hannah

Platirius: Infiltration Book I
Platirius: The Rise of Reve Book II
Platirius: Kikhani vs Platirius Book III
Coldarius: The Origin of Gallium Book I
Coldarius: The Betrayal Book II
JanIus: Pawns Book I
JanIus: Enter the King Book II
JanIus: Platirius vs JanIus Book III
Maieman: Paradox Book I
Maieman: Revelations Book II

www.ingramcontent.com/pod-product-compliance
Lightning Source LLC
Chambersburg PA
CBHW072228190626
46809CB00017B/1526